A STRANGER CAME BY

ALANNA KNIGHT

A Stranger Came By

HURST & BLACKETT

HURST & BLACKETT LTD

3 Fitzroy Square, London W.1.

An Imprint of the Hutchinson Publishing Group

London Melbourne Sydney Auckland
Wellington Johannesburg Cape Town
and agencies throughout the world

First published 1974
© Alanna Knight 1974

$\frac{F}{5}$

639305

Printed in Great Britain by
Flarepath Printers Ltd, St. Albans, Herts.
and bound by Wm Brendon & Son,
Tiptree, Essex

ISBN 0 09 121610 9

To
JOAN LINGARD
with love

1

'Poison Trial Verdict Today – All the latest – '

Through the narrow window far above my head, Edinburgh was a fragment of cloud drifting lazily across a patch of blue sky on an early spring day. From beyond these stone walls floated the echoes of its High Street, the sounds of carriage wheels on cobbles with the street vendors calling their wares and the chirping shrillness of newsboys:

'On Trial for Her Life – Read all about it.'

And as if in certainty of the melancholy conclusion, a lone piper practised a lament. Imagination soared to the castle battlements on a windy day, until the sound grew louder and erupted as a pipe band marching down the Royal Mile towards Holyrood Palace, where presumably there were celebrations following the recent Royal Wedding of the Duke of Connaught to Princess Margaret of Prussia.

As the sound died my mind took wings and flew over the miles to quiet Monkshall. On a day like this dust-moted sunlight would caress neglected staircases and die against oak-panelled walls, its only life a trapped insect beating against the glass of the shuttered windows. An empty mansion standing in that forlorn and empty landscape which separates Edinburgh from the cold North Sea.

A key turned in the lock jolting me into the grim present. Would *he* be there in court, waiting?

Edinburgh, Monkshall, and a strange man in a green great-coat. Had I been sure of a future I might have searched the world and found no sweeter dream.

But now the grim face of my gaoler indicated by a curt nod

that it was time, and my footsteps echoed along the corridors beside him. Time – time – how little I have left of you. Then suddenly through a high window I saw that the roofs were wet and shining. Rain. Rain on one's face – how sweet the memory. A door opened somewhat ahead of us and I fancied the sudden breeze carried the smell of it, fresh and soft, from the Pentland Hills. I thought I heard the seagulls too, hovering noisily inland towards Monkshall, but it was the rough voice at my side:

'Hurry along there. What are ye stopping for?'

Another door and the twittering of birds in the walled garden at Monkshall became the distant sound of the courtroom's audience eagerly awaiting today's sensations.

Would my stranger be there too, sitting in his accustomed seat?

Three days ago all those faces which had become familiar had been obliterated when I found the eyes of the man in the green greatcoat watching me intently, as I took my place in the dock. Not that such action was in itself surprising. Accused of murdering my guardian and employer, I was the main attraction the Edinburgh Court had put on in some considerable time.

On trial for my life, alas, even my looks were against me, for they were without a doubt those popularly depicting the villainess in illustrated romances. Where custom and fashion supposed goodness and virtue to be associated with fair young virgins, soft of eye with rosebud mouths, I was nearing thirty, tall and gawky in an unBritish way, with dense black hair, a too-wide mouth, swarthy skin and large fierce dark eyes. In similar circumstances a hundred years earlier, Christina Holly – *even* the name was outlandish and alien – would have doubtless burnt as a witch.

Just as the finality of death had its grades of horror, I thought with a shudder, the rope's end more merciful than slow burning, or as news of the distant war reached our newspapers, the torture of a Zulu spear.

No, it was certainly not my beauty that arrested the strange man's attention and his eyes held more than the ghoulish sexual interest of a particular kind of man. His eyes communicated. It was as if, over the learned heads, the seas of words, those steady eyes questioned destiny, sent their silent message of hope in despair or love with tenderness, as if for a little while our spirits walked together far from this grim scene to some wooded glade and mountain path where clear streams murmured. He was neither particularly handsome nor particularly young. His hair was the colour of the wet sand at ebb-tide. It curled into sideburns and a thick strand bleached paler than the rest fell boyishly straight over a high forehead. Wide cheekbones threw harsh shadows on to a lean jaw, emphasising a craggy face that kept its own council and held its own secrets. Here was a countenance unaccustomed to much ready mirth, I thought, and composed entirely of angles would please only a sculptor.

My eyes had scrutinised him boldly with interest unashamed, for who knew how little time remained for indulgence of my senses at the sight of an attractive man. It was then I noticed that his mouth was large, the lips voluptuous, so as to be at complete odds with that stern and brooding face. The mouth of a sensualist and the first complexity. For among young ladies who read novelettes or swooned over Mr. Heathcliff, here was Mr. Rochester to the life.

Tastefully dressed, he emanated the well-bred poise of the rich. As he stood up at the end of the session, buttoning his greatcoat, I also saw that he was almost a head taller than anyone else in the room. He was there the next day and the next and it was because of his presence that I missed much of the vital evidence, mumbling self-consciously, surprised at the onslaught of this man upon my emotions. Surprised too that my passion for the actor Willy Tyler which had precipitated me into this catastrophe, could have evaporated so speedily as to seem mere caprice and left me so vulnerable.

I was sufficiently excited by this stranger with whom I

9

would never exchange a single word to anticipate his arrival by indulging in a fantasy. Seeing him breakfasting in a large mansion, waited upon by servants, reading the newspaper. There was no one seated across the table from him. I felt sure that like myself, he was alone and unhappy. Imagination painted no wife into this domestic scene. I saw him look at his watch, call for his carriage –

And there was absolutely no excuse for my behaviour. After all I should have learned the dangers that lurked with attractive men. My mother's gipsy blood was no doubt re-asserting itself and in a resurgence of some female vanity I had thought lost for ever when this grim justice shut me away from the decent law-abiding world, I bit my lips violently to give them redness and as we approached the courtroom I deplored what I could do nothing about. The prison pallor, the dull lankness of hair, neglected, unwashed at least it was thick and dense enough to conceal its lack-lustre. Most of all, I deplored the lack of fresh linen which gave my hideous coarse dress this lived-in smell. I thought with longing of those weekly baths and hair-washings which even the servants at Monkshall endured, not always without indignation, obeying often mutinously Sir Andrew Howe's rigid code of hygiene, and dismissing their employer as a 'daft old fanatic'.

As I took my place in the dock, I was almost afraid to raise my eyes, and when I did so I realised my miserable attempts at self-improvement had been in vain. He wasn't there. Hopefully I watched and waited, then in a despair I did not expect to find remaining among my torn-out emotions, I realised he had been no more than an interested spectator. A woman on trial was more fun that cock-fighting or any of the barbarous amusements where well-to-do gentlemen could still find illicit pleasure. Had I not detected a streak of cruelty in that face and Heaven only guessed what vicarious excite-ment in those intimate glances we had shared.

I told myself angrily that he had been nothing but a sensa-tion-seeker, waiting for all his apparent refinement for the salacious details, as avidly as any of the lewd faces in the gallery.

The court rose as Lord Deas, the judge, entered. Reporters resumed their eager scribbling as they struggled for words to describe the accused woman's face as the court reassembled.

Frowning, they watched me. Would she hang or no? Did she care?

I fancied the words would read: 'Her demeanour as the verdict of Guilty was delivered and the judge placed upon his head the melancholy black cap –' For that was the verdict the press anxiously awaited, of that I had not the least doubt. Nor could I blame them for being human and having jobs to keep by writing a good dramatic story. For despite the preachings and teachings of church and society, alas, in this life dramas are not made nor newspapers sold by man's innocence or woman's virtue.

I had given them little copy so far. I was not even a beautiful temptress, a seductive Jezebel, but only a plain spinster, no longer young. And had my reactions been sought by these same reporters scribbling away for dear life I should have admitted that personally I found 'the accused' and her crime both extremely dull. After the initial curiosity and terror of standing trial, I found myself regarding the whole proceedings with the utmost indifference and detachment. It was as if I had read an account of it all long ago and far from absorbing all my attentions as it should, my mind continually wandered as if I listened to a long-winded and particularly dreary sermon and my most earnest desire became the wish that they would get over this tedious assault upon my senses as swiftly as possible.

Perhaps posterity would remember only that my mother was a gipsy, a point which had been often stressed during these last few days and society would blame it all upon her, whose only misdemeanour had been to bring me into the world. My boredom would be dismissed as the inbuilt resignation and fatalism of the lower classes, 'dull, witless and only fit to serve their betters'. I remembered my frequent yawns for the room was close and hot with trapped sunlight, and how eyes had watched and pencils busily recorded them, while the jury too thoughtfully noted that such heartless behaviour tokened indifference and arrogance, and would weigh it in their own balance.

I must take care for such yawns could cost me my life. So might amused smiles at some bewigged pomposity be written off as grossest cynicism which would go down ill with the jurymen. I was reaping a bitter harvest of living long with a man who had taught me to laugh at affectations, in myself as well as others.

A shaft of sunlight slid across my shoulders like a gentle arm's caress, with a tenderness that brought vividly the sensation of life flooding through me, each artery, each finger alive, each pore bursting with life. Tears pricked at my eyes. Why should this be happening to me when I was innocent, victim of a jealous woman's greed?

Stop. Stop. Suddenly I wanted to scream the word, over and over. For in spite of all that had gone before. I could not believe that this was other than the enactment of some contrived drama I watched, with actors poor and stilted words spoken concerning that fate of Christina Holly. Most of all, should the day go ill, I could not believe that at the end of it, someone would tighten a rope about my neck and a trap door would open. A step, then the eternity of nothing.

'To sum up briefly' (began Prosecution) 'Sir Andrew Howe is dead –'

To sum up briefly was something of which the court was incapable and to save my patient reader the tedium of long-winded 'heretofores' and 'inasmuches' I will endeavour to shortly outline the events which had led me to this fatal hour.

*   *   *   *

Of my parentage nothing is known and my early life was spent in a torment of speculation as to who might have been

12

my father. My mother was a gipsy dancer, free with her love as her graceful movement, with the result that she arrived at Monkshall in a storm one Christmas Eve and bore me alone in the stable at midnight. No star in the east, no Magi appeared to mark this blasphemy of the Divine Nativity, only Sir Andrew wondering at the commotion among his horses. He was in time to rescue me from the side of my mother who thereupon paid her debt to the society whose code she had flaunted by considerately dying in his arms. Poor Sir Andrew. His wife had died six months previously in medically similar but physically more comfortable circumstances and despite assurances that the babe was 'the Devil's work' he decided, after exhaustive and fruitless enquiries to raise me as his own ward, much to the disgust of his step-daughter Edith who was then twelve years old and keen to have me delivered to whatever gipsies could be found. Edith, in fact, might have served as the model for one of Cinderella's step-sisters in every way but looks. She was far from ugly except in nature, her beauty was a local legend and she soon became the object of rich and eligible suitors, one of whom, Sir Samuel Browne, carried her off to his Border castle a little before my sixth birthday.

So it was that 'Christina Holly', as Sir Andrew fancifully called me on account of the holly-bush outside the front door being the first thing my infant eyes beheld with a smile, took her somewhat uneasy place half-daughter, half-servant, while eager ladies – with an eye on Sir Andrew as a prospective husband – rushed to hand me pamphlets as soon as I could read. They sought to save me, to secure my soul, while the more ignorant superstitious females in the locality made the sign against witches when I passed by, regarding the gross mimicry of my nativity as my first step on the path back to damnation and the Devil from whence I had come.

Let us return for a moment to the Edinburgh court-room –

Dr. Littlejohn has just taken the stand and testified: 'I have

13

been police surgeon in Edinburgh for twenty-five years.' Cross-examined he has stated 'I am satisfied that the dose of laudanum found in the contents of the deceased's stomach was enough to cause death.'

Prosecution after some learned discourse has informed us: 'What the jury must now decide is whether this was self-administered or by the accused.'

Not by me, I swear I am innocent. I loved, respected Sir Andrew whatever the court and his greedy stepdaughter tried to prove. The kind guardian of childhood, the gentle counsellor of girlhood who made me see so clearly when suitors came along how *unsuitable* they were. How this one had the makings of a drunken sot, that one a bore, that one the mark of a fortune-hunter. So the marriageable years passed until less than a year ago, I began to understand the horrifying reason why my guardian had denied me a ward's right to marry.

Many were the tormented hours I spent in my cell reliving the possible causes of abrupt change in behaviour, seeing in the past year how he would watch me, smiling tenderly, head-on-side, with a young lover's eyes hungrily appraising from an old man's face. Caressing my hand, my hair, so that always afraid to incite him to further liberties and rebuffs, I would seek refuge in a cold distant manner, keeping always the length of a table, some piece of furniture between us, a door for ready escape.

Even then I despised myself for the unfair advantage I had over him in youth's swift movement of retreat, conscious too that my chilly detachment only inflamed his desire, and drove him to the degradation of passionate pleadings, of tears.

'Marry me, marry me, Christina.' But I could not marry him. 'But you will – perhaps not tomorrow – in a little while, when you get used to the idea of your guardian also as your husband.'

How could I ever get used to such a preposterous idea? How could the impersonal dull-eyed jury be expected to believe my story that delicacy, even decency, forbade marriage to a besotted old gentleman whom I had been brought up to regard as father, protector and guardian. Surely to only the most insensitive could refusal of such a marriage with all its material advantages appear like crass ingratitude?

Strangely enough, Sir Andrew in his more lucid moments, would have understood and applauded the decision of a gipsy brat's refusal to marry her rich and respected guardian. 'This modern society of hypocrites,' he had called it, 'where parents sold daughters as readily as any African savage, their currency priced not in cows but in elegant mansions and tempting dowries.' Marriage without love would have reduced me to the ranks of fortune-hunters whom he had taught me to despise. He had encouraged and helped develop my sense of romance and romance bred delicacy.

What brought about this change in him? His motives must forever remain hidden. Perhaps believing himself to be near death made him desperate for the love of a wife – and a child – to prove his own immortality. But that I shudder to remember. Evenings that had earlier been devoted to reading to each other the novels of Sir Walter Scott or Mr. William Thackeray or the latest contributions to literature which had been favourably reviewed in *The Scotsman* were suddenly replaced by his desire to sit close and holding my hand, discuss the future he had planned for us. Once certain that I was about to change my mind, he confessed that he had deliberately spurned my earlier suitors, humiliated them, made them outrageous in my eyes. When I asked him why, he had smiled:

'Because your intellect, my dear, which I myself created, had to be saved for someone worthy. Of course, had such a young man revealed himself I would not have stood in your way. But consider the young men of today –' After shaking his head sadly, he had continued: 'How could I watch that fine brain wasted, see you becoming a mere chattel, a breeding machine.' Placing the tips of his fingers together he added thoughtfully: 'It must have been ten years ago, at least, when

I realised that I myself could not have wished for a better mate, and from that day I continued your education with the express purpose of making you my wife –'

So night after night, I listened with growing horror, to the ravings of this Pygmalion to whom I had been an unsuspecting Galatea, as he often repeated: 'Of course, my love, I had to bide my time, give you every chance to manage your own life. It was only when I saw that your marriageable years had passed that I realised the workings of fate had intended you should be my bride. Why else do you think I have patiently endured being a widower?'

And he would talk in some clinical detail of my providing the son he had longed for, unaware that I listened in silent agonies, longing to be away to shut my ears, still loving and respecting him, but with the idea of such intimacies as sharing his bed, his body, utterly repellent and even incestuous. Perhaps my attitude was mistaken for modesty for to my further embarrassment he pressed upon me a series of manuals regarding the sexual functions: Sex and Love in Marriage; Love not Lust; The Female Role in Sex Gratification. He earnestly requested that I should read these and several more and discuss anything I found difficult to understand so that he could enlighten me further.

These manuals I thrust away at the back of a drawer out of Mrs. Maxwell's sight as I had once before on the eve of my thirteenth birthday, when a book explaining the change from girl to woman appeared on my bedside table. Mrs. Maxwell putting away clean linen had discovered it and the mother of some seven daughters, three of whom survived, had said to me sternly: 'I hadna need for books with diagrams, ye ken, to explain to my lassies where babies came from. It's a perfectly natural procedure and what the Good Lord intended us for, so with your permission I'll take the liberty of explaining it to you.' She did so and I never saw the offending book again.

Alas, I could hardly explain my present predicament to

Mrs. Maxwell. That I could not marry good Sir Andrew and had my life depended on it I could never live with him as his wife. And so it came that my life did depend on it, for had Sir Andrew married me and had an heir, Lady Edith would have been disinherited and he would have left me – if the story of the mysterious disease were true – in due course, a rich and respected widow.

Poor Sir Andrew. I have heard since that often men turn lecherous in old age and afraid of advancing years and increased debility, fight a forlorn battle to keep time at bay. Age is something that happens to other men, they tell their mirrors every day, the clock's relentless progress will never wither *them*. Yet through all this agony of emotions, he remained basically my kind guardian, the stern but considerate employer of the staff at Monkshall.

Maybe I would not have fallen so readily in love with Willy Tyler had I not seen his advent into my life at the height of Sir Andrew's passion, as a means of escape. Surely if he saw me in love with a young and eligible man the folly of his own feelings would become apparent and he would swiftly return to my avuncular image of him. Such an ending, alas, suitable for a Restoration play, was not the case. The very reverse was true and my infatuation for Willy merely added flame to fire and jealously to an old man's passion.

Matters came to a head that fatal Christmas of 1878. Lady Edith and her husband Sir Samuel came to stay and we went to see the pantomime of The Sleeping Beauty at the Royal Princess Theatre, dining afterwards at the Café Royal. Willy Tyler meanwhile was appearing in recitations from the Immortal Bard as part of the variety programme at Cook's Royal Circus, in Lothian Road. And the following day being a Sunday I asked him to dine with us. Everything seemed to be going splendidly when perhaps at the instigation of too much wine freely imbibed the whole pleasurable meal erupted into a hideous scene of raised tempers, angry words, recriminations.

17

Of this scene, the Browne servants were sole witnesses, for traditionally once the meal was on the table at this time of year, all the Monkshall servants were sent home to the village to enjoy whatever time and leftovers from the festive board remained, with their families. With the tragedy complete, the Monkshall servants could only testify to my hitherto good character and tighten the noose about my neck by confirming Sir Andrew's deep love of me.

'If I cannot have you, then no one else shall –' Had he actually uttered those words as the servants claimed? I had no remembrance of them but the Browne servants apparently had their ears glued to the drawing-room door throughout, anxious not to miss a single word. They could and did remember and in some detail. The evidence sounded remarkably like an episode from the somewhat naïve melodramas Willy Tyler was touring around Scotland when our paths crossed at Miss Meade's soirée at Craighall. Miss Meade was our local patroness of the arts, her drawing-room for ever seething with handsome but often hopeless actors, clowns who saw themselves as Hamlets, or King Lears who behaved like clowns. Scandal whispered that her sister Madeline, patroness of another art, was known to recruit her lovers also from Craighall.

'But facts are chiels that winna ding' – words of Robert Burns that Sir Andrew was fond of quoting. And facts remained. The morning after that fatal dinner-party, Sir Andrew was dead. I found him, and the note on the table beside him:

My dearest, I shall always love you. Do what you will. In life and death your devoted Servant.

Snatching it up I ran to Edith's bedroom. Half-an-hour later the doctor's carriage arrived and a little later he pronounced Sir Andrew's death as due to an overdose of laudanum.

'He took his own life,' I said weeping.

'Have you evidence?' asked the doctor.

'Yes, he left a note.'

'Then fetch it, if you please,' he said quietly.

Moments later I stood there foolishly insisting that there *had been* a note, which had vanished completely, while Edith and her husband stood grim-faced throughout, their silence only broken to deny all knowledge of a note's existence. Looks were exchanged, the doctor said:

'You know then that the procurator fiscal must be informed. There will have to be an investigation.'

The investigation led to my arrest on suspicion of murder where perhaps the most agonising part was Edith's base betrayal. What I had regarded through the years as jealousy erupted into a concealed passion of loathing and fear that her stepfather's fortune would by-pass them and fall into the hands of a mere servant. I wondered many times at what stage of that fatal morning they exchanged glances, crumpled and burnt the suicide note, knowing full well that by so doing they condemned an innocent woman, whom they had known since her childhood, to death and how after I was dead, they would live with their terrible consciences.

Sir Andrew had taught me to regard all men as equals. Servant and master had equal rights as human beings. I could not believe that the Brownes regarded me as belonging to some inferior and different species, but so much was evident from their statements. The domestic was a kind of sub-human. What did it matter to employers, for I belonged to those lower classes to whom unfortunate things happened regularly, things like poverty, overwork, early deaths. They dismissed Sir Andrew's guardianship as a poor joke. I was merely an upstart gipsy brat who had mesmerised her employer into loving her.

Member of Parliament, Justice of the Peace, a pillar of the church and Edinburgh society, the newspapers were inclined to believe good Sir Samuel. I was also marked down as ungrateful for hadn't Lady Edith by showing marked charity in discarded clothes and footwear lavished upon me the care of a sister?

As the Browne servants testified to the angry quarrel, their exaggerations stimulated I suspected by prospects of a wage increase, the Monkshall maids tearful and scared out of their wits yet anxious to please and Mrs. Maxwell desperate to prove how greatly Sir Andrew loved me and my utter devotion to him, all fell into the neat traps laid for them by the prosecution and made the evidence of my guilt complete.

'Sir Samuel and other witnesses present that fatal night have testified that Sir Andrew threatened to cut the accused out of his will if she married the actor Willy Tyler – '

And with the note that could have saved me also vanished Willy, scuttling away to freedom, I thought bitterly. Without Sir Andrew's fortune what use had he for me?

'Much has been made by defence of some mysterious disease the ravages of which Sir Andrew feared, hints of a tumour of the brain have been made. We have before us the learned doctor's evidence that there was in fact, no trace of any such disease. We also have the evidence of his lawyers and bankers, his personal friends – all have testified to his robust health, his plans for the future. I ask the court, would any man of Sir Andrew's intelligence and knowledge, contemplate suicide while furthering such plans for the future? And now I must ask the court who stood to gain by his death – '

The person who stood to gain by *my* death was Edith, but to hint at such a miscarriage of human nature filled the court with virtuous horror. His late wife's daughter or the accused – a mere servant who had wheedled him into parting with his fortune to her?

'Is not blood thicker than water?' thundered Prosecution, and might well have added : 'Are not riches and social position more convincing of Christian goodness and virtue than the dubious birthright of a foundling child?'

I leave my readers to their own conclusions and digress to inspect my audience in that grim courtroom. I knew them well. The sensation seekers, the curious, those who merely came in for a welcome seat away from the chilly spring sunshine of Edinburgh's High Street. The poor without money for fuel, the destitute without shelter. Then there were the ghouls, the descendants of those who had taken their children to watch some poor wretch die in agony at the Tolbooth and regarded it as a holiday, a reason for celebration. Last of all, the salacious avidly awaiting intimate details and – so far – disappointed that none had been revealed.

The same people in the same places each day. I felt I should acknowledge their presence with a polite greeting for I had reached the stage of interested speculation should any of these familiar faces be absent. What catastrophe had overwhelmed the man with the strawberry nose, or the bird-eyed woman with her knitting like a latter-day Madame Defarge from Mr. Dickens' novel? As for the judge, the learned counsels, I was merely a cipher, a case to them, to be laid aside with the wigs and gowns at the end of the day, my unfortunate image soon erased by good wine and excellent beef.

In the silence as the jury adjourned, an insect trapped on some nearby window, a captive like myself, buzzed despairingly. I remembered that there had been a house-fly trapped in Sir Andrew's bedroom the morning I found him dead. Christmas flies were lucky, said gipsy lore. But not for me. Bad luck, good luck, how easily my gipsy forbears had simplified life into two compartments.

Good luck. If my stranger in the green greatcoat had come, he might have brought me luck –

And if the verdict were in my favour where would I go when I left this place? What roads existed led into a shadowy future, wherever I walked whatever I did, my past would be the spectre that haunted me, always ready and eager to appear. I was quite capable of being a governess but who would care to put their children in the care of a possible murderess? If I had done to death my kind employer and guardian, what scant mercies could I be expected to show their precious babes?

Nor was marriage left to me either. What respectable man would wish to introduce me to his family with the word: 'This is Miss Christina Holly, you remember, Mama she was lately in the news concerning the death of her guardian, Sir Andrew Howe'.

Only some man with a morbid distortion of natural affections, some debased creature eager for sensation would wish to embrace Christina Holly, a possible murderess. And then, what of the day when he felt a little unwell? What if some bout of sickness should strike him unexpectedly? Would not his mind automatically wander to an old man dead from an overdose of laudanum? Would he not tremble as he watched me move silently about the house, interpreting silence as some secret sinister intent and fall to thinking of certain material possessions I stood to gain by his demise?

My gloomy reverie was interrupted by a ripple of excitement, the handing over of a paper, the sudden recalling of the jury. The court's sombre atmosphere was shattered by excited murmurs and craning of heads.

'My lord, I beg leave to call another witness,' said council for the defence. He glanced at me for the first time with something like animation as the court resounded to the calling for:

'William Tyler!'

2

In total disbelief, I watched Willy Tyler stroll down to the witness box, bowing slightly as he progressed, as though already on stage before an admiring audience. He took the oath in the same ringing tones I had last heard him declaim Hamlet's soliloquy. When asked why he had not appeared sooner, he stated blandly that he had but yesterday returned from a successful tour in the United States of America. On reading the newspapers, he had of course set forth immediately for the Edinburgh Court.

He avoided looking in my direction.

In a dream-like stupor I watched the face I had thought so handsome. Dark eyes that once appeared bright and dancing now seemed shifty. And was there not something wolfish about his too-eager smile? Surely what I had once considered elegance was merely the shallow frippery of flamboyance. Almost against my will I found myself comparing him to the stranger in the green greatcoat with his airs of breeding, the sort of man who would never care what he looked like, yet would instinctively lend grace and elegance to the meanest of clothes.

I found I was leaning forward anxiously wondering what he could possibly say at this late stage to avert the catastrophe that my life had become. And I considered with growing alarm the effect his flashy appearance might have on that dull and conservative jury. With what impression other than an ill one, would his mysterious new evidence be received, for as he had departed from Monkshall some hours before Sir Andrew's death and left the country presumably before my arrest, I could not see any contribution from him of a worthwhile nature. He answered the routine questions put to him in a civil voice which still maintained its quality of rich brown velvet. The darling of many women in his time, he made an immediate impact on the females in the audience. Their sighs were clearly audible.

Council for the defence was begging leave to inform the court: 'According to evidence given hitherto, Lady Edith Browne had looked in at midnight to say goodnight to her stepfather. She was the last to see him alive, for according to medical evidence Sir Andrew died in the early hours of the following morning and the overdose of laudanum was taken sometime after midnight. It has been established that the accused was in her room with the door locked from eight o'clock when she fled the dinner-table after the infamous quarrel when Mr. Tyler left the house.' He paused dramatically looked around the court.

'I am now to establish that this was mere delicacy on the accused's part and that she was not in fact, in the house at all.'

'Have you evidence in support of this statement?'

'I have, m'lord, and I call upon Mr. Willy Tyler to give testimony.'

'Pray proceed, Mr. Tyler.'

'My lord, the young lady was considerably upset by Sir Andrew's behaviour and as I left the house, called to me from an upstairs window and begged that I take her with me for staying in the house was intolerable to her. I waited for a few moments and she appeared from the side door which leads into the courtyard –' He hesitated, his eyelids fluttering towards the crowded gallery leaning forward so as not to miss a word.

'Proceed.'

With a sigh and apparent reluctance, he continued: 'The young lady spent the night with me at the Juniper Arms.'

The twitterings from the gallery became an uproar of delighted 'oh's' and 'ah's' at this unexpected piece of scandal,

24

for the Juniper Arms disguised as a hostelry on the Glasgow Road was a well-known house of assignation. Willy Tyler had told me of its reputation himself and the truth of that statement was now clearly substantiated by the court's reaction.

Unable to contain my anger at such perjury and regardless of the consequences of denial, I tried to rush forward shouting:

'It's a lie – it isn't true. It's a lie – '

Rough hands seized my arms and I realised the uselessness of denial even if the noisy court would have listened. As the court was called sharply to order I thought, who would believe me, anyway, when they wanted to believe Willy Tyler.

In the silence Willy Tyler cleared his throat delicately. 'Next morning, however, I awoke to find that the young lady was already dressed and weeping copiously. She announced that she was most concerned about Sir Andrew and wished to return to Monkshall with all possible speed, to be reconciled to him. I have not seen her again until this moment.'

'Have you any – er, witness – to this – um, night in the Juniper Arms, Mr. Tyler?'

'I have indeed.'

John and Sarah Selby were called. A fat painted middle-aged woman, an obvious madame, waddled to the witness box followed by a coarse brutal faced man, with the scars of an ex-pugilist. They announced themselves as proprietors of the Juniper Arms and with a brazen indifference to perjury, proceeded to swear on oath that Mr. Tyler and a young lady: 'Yes, your honour, the lady in the dock, the very same' – spent the night in question in Room 6 of their establishment. They had taken the liberty of bringing their account book which was passed round and an entry read aloud that Mr. Willy Tyler and wife, had paid six shillings for bed and breakfast in their room.

'But it isn't true – it wasn't me. It wasn't me.' But no one believed or even listened. Salacious knowing eyes, lewd grins were turned in my direction. Necks were craned from the gallery followed by a certain amount of pushing and disorderly standing on benches for a closer look which was quelled instantly by a call to 'Order, order' and a threat to 'clear the court'.

My rejection of perjured evidence was taken as a nice piece of false modesty. Naturally a young woman of any breeding would prefer even death to losing her self respect by publicly admitting that she spent the night in a brothel with an actor.

The jury again retired and after a short absence returned by a majority of one a verdict of 'Not proven'. The result of this verdict was received by a cheer and some cat-calls from the occupants of the gallery.

My face burning with shame I left the dock, a free woman and for all the wrong reasons. And if I knew any relief at all, it was because the man in the green greatcoat had not been present to witness my humiliation. I had a strange feeling that those dark eyes could burn with scorn and mockery.

*   *   *   *

Next day I returned to Monkshall. I would have preferred some place less haunting, less steeped in bitter memory, but there was nowhere else to go. This great empty mansion belonged to me under the terms of Sir Andrew's will. The remainder of the estate had gone to Lady Edith but as her stepfather had lived and died an ardent philanthropist and collector of lost causes, most of his money had appropriately vanished during his lifetime in impossible investments. If there was satisfaction to be gained, then it was in the sole thought that the mere pittance remaining must have caused those wily plotters, the Brownes, some severe gnashing of teeth.

And Monkshall too must go under the hammer. For even had I wished to live in a large melancholy mansion all alone, I had no money for its upkeep.

As I left the Portobello coach at its gates, I wondered a

little selfconsciously if eyes followed my progress and whether any of the passengers associated me with the infamies that had lately blazoned across their newspapers. Presumably not, for no inquisitive eyes turned in my direction, nor did my fellow-travellers stir from their apathetic ruminations. Besides Monkshall did not advertise itself unduly. The house was obscure and well hidden behind a high garden wall, approached by a narrow entrance and a drive that twisted away through an abundance of trees.

As I hurried down the drive clutching my valise containing the few possessions I had taken with me, I saw that the world had indeed moved on. Winter had still reigned when I made my last dramatic exit, the trees were stark and bare. Now spring green and warm sunshine seeped through their boughs. Daffodils grew everywhere, thick clumps that seemed to lift bright heads and nod encouragingly as I passed by. A mere fancy, of course, but heartening, even if only the breeze moved them into what my starved life craved at such a moment – the semblance of attitudes of smiling welcome from someone – or something.

A slight movement on a branch above my head, followed by a pair of bright eyes and a red squirrel stared down. I had to laugh, for I had seen that curious expression so many times of late and it took me right back into the courtroom. I stopped, clapped my hands at the sudden delight of being free and alive, able to live the rest of my life without fear.

Free. Free to live. And I laughed aloud and danced a few wild steps. With a look reproachful as any outraged spinster, at this unseemly merriment, my squirrel departed huffily, tail bouncing indignantly along into the hollow of his tree.

'Oh, come back – you silly – please come back. I didn't mean to frighten you.' I would have been the most surprised person in the entire world had he obeyed my command. 'Oh, never mind then.'

I was so happy, glad to be home and I felt again that sense of being welcomed and protected by the great trees of Monkshall. Massive, old and strong, it needed less vivid imagination than mine to see that thus they had looked on the day when the ancient abbey which Monkshall had replaced was sacked and its monks scattered. I touched the warm solid bark of an oak, wrinkled, scarred with age. Did a heart beat inside against my hand?

Suddenly I wanted to remain here, outside, with these impersonal trees in the garden where I was free. I had no desire to go alone into that silent waiting house, to be enclosed by a locked door and strong stone walls. I laid my face against the sun-warmed wood of the ancient doorway, around which insects murmured among the early shrubs. Trees and house in that moment seemed to converge, to become the very texture of eternity, as if they whispered:

'We have suffered and endured – you also – you also – '

Avoiding the courtyard with its stables and the fifteenth century cottage above where the housekeeper Mrs. Maxwell used to live, I walked quickly down the side path leading through the rose garden to the front of the house. Buds quickened on every thorny shoot and the first leaves were red as blood. Above my head the shuttered windows seemed devoid of all life and I stopped, remembering how in November, I had walked here at Sir Andrew's side, gathering the last roses, while he directed the gardener in his autumn tasks.

Looking up at the sky that day, I had felt a cloud slide over the sun, and instantly experienced a moment's giddiness as if the world was off its axis, out of phase. Time itself slid ahead like a clock gone mad with the hands spinning. Then it was over. Everything was as it had been before except that the moment had left me vulnerable to terrors unspecified.

I had smelt tragedy in the wind that morning and now recognised too late the significance of my gipsy blood. I wondered if my mother had told fortunes as well as dancing for men's love, for I had seen disaster's stealthy approach and as if the words had been clearly written across the sky, I had known that Sir Andrew would never see these roses bloom again.

My footsteps carried me to the magnificent front of the house with its prospect of lawns, formal garden and on a clear day from the upstairs windows, the straight eternal line of the North Sea. As I let myself out by the wrought iron gate a rose bush dragged at my skirt like a ghostly hand beseeching me to remain in the past. I shivered, dragged it protesting away. The once smooth lawns were unkempt, sullied after winter storms, brown and peevish with withered leaves everywhere. Before me, the great curved flight of stone steps still swept gracefully down from the drawing-room but they were neglected, overgrown with a tangle of briars. Blue skies and warm sun had vanished into the sombre grey of a threatening storm. A heavy sky above, all around me the heavy silence of desolation turned this into a house from the legend of the Sleeping Beauty, a place forgotten, dead as its owners, with eyes shuttered against the passage of time.

The walled garden with its memories was not to be faced just then. Footsteps faltered before the sundial, the small arbors with their dreams of the laughter of childhood, with Mrs. Maxwell, far above my head in those days, carrying tea on a tray into the languid summer garden. Then with the playthings of childhood abandoned into the dusty attics, came girlhood with the adored man who cherished and protected me. Good kind Sir Andrew the idol who had changed without warning, Beauty's Prince into Beast, whose friendly merry eyes had gleamed with the hunger of lust, whose hands no longer avuncular moved with the power and strength of a frightening unwanted suitor.

Cold now with a wind stronger than the approaching storm that blew into Monkshall from a grey sea eight miles distant, I hurried across the lawn and completing the circuit entered the courtyard from the garden side. The stables were behind me, silent and forlorn. Today there would be no friendly whickering or stamp of foot from Fortune or Ladybelle. I wondered sadly where they had gone, who were their new owners.

I took out my key, approached the door. Suddenly there

was a sound behind me. Unbelievingly I listened, turned, ran across the cobbles and threw open the stable door.

'Oh, you darling – oh Ladybelle, my love. Oh, my beautiful Fortune – '

Finding relief in tears, I stayed with them, dabbing at my eyes, talking, asking them – as if they were capable of answer – who had tended them so well and what they were doing at Monkshall all alone? Obligingly they nibbled hay from my hand, snorting down my neck warmly, nuzzling my pockets for the goodies I once carried. At last, half-in-laughter, half-in-tears, I closed the door and went into Monkshall.

Even expectation paled before the reality before me. I had not been prepared for its tomb-like silence, its vast emptiness, as if – as if the feeling of death itself had spread into every corner. I wandered from room to room on tiptoe, a little reverently as if I was indeed in the presence of the dead. But everything once familiar now stood alien, aloof, all that I had loved and touched was dust-sheeted, remote. The beautiful alive house had retreated from me for ever. Each room as I opened its door seemed to shudder away, as if scandalised by the disgrace I had brought upon this house. One after another I closed doors gently behind me until I was back downstairs in the hall, drawing on my gloves. I must leave immediately, the thought of staying in the face of such – hostility – was a physical impossibility. How could I hope to breathe life into this desert of shrouded furniture, shuttered rooms? The prospect was nauseating, utterly beyond what I had expected, a house where the very walls shrank from me. At that moment I gave way to despair, I sat down and cried, for none would ever know that Monkshall itself had finally broken my heart.

Footsteps and warm arms gathered me to an ample bosom. I looked up into the face of Mrs. Maxwell.

'Miss, miss, you should have told me you was coming. There's nothing in the house – but I can give you bacon and egg at the cottage. Come away, come away – '

A child again, after a scolding for some mild misdemeanour,

I allowed her to lead me across the courtyard, up the spiral stairs into the cottage above the stables. Drying my eyes, I sat down obediently and watched while she breathed life into glowing coals in the massive fireplace, then as bacon sizzled in a large frying pan, she said she had just that moment returned from tending the hens some of whom had wandered and their eggs took such a time to gather. When had I arrived? By the time the table was set and I was enjoying my third slice of bread newly baked that morning, she told me she hadn't gone with the others when they left.

'I always believed you would come back to the house, ye ken – and I couldna' bear to part wi' the horses. I told them a lie, said they were your horses and there could be no talk of disposing of them until – ' she avoided my eyes – 'until all that other business was over and done wi'.' She handed me a copy of *The Scotsman*. 'I don't hold much wi' newspaper-reading, but Miss Meade up at Craighall, knowing I've been concerned, has been giving her copy to my lassie Sarah – she's companion, ye'll mind – '

I needed no reminder that during Willy Tyler's stay with Miss Meade, Sarah had been the means of exchanging messages and love tokens.

'Is it all there?' I gulped. 'Everything?'

Mrs. Maxwell cleared her throat. 'It is, miss, but I ken fine it's all lies. Why, you were in the house when I came over at six that morning, in your bed when I brought your breakfast and you couldna' possibly have got back all those miles from Glasgow Road without carriage or horse and me not seen or heard you coming down the drive. If you remember I was up most of the night wi' my wee grandson's toothache, he stayed wi' me while his mammy was lying-in – I'd never have believed it of you anyway, miss, not the way you was brought up.'

I threw down the paper. 'Then why did he do it?'

'To save your life, miss. The gentleman did what he could and he didna' have much time to be choosy. Sichlike people as keep places like yon will do anything for money.' She

31

paused. 'Dinna ye worry – I know the truth but ye can rely on me. I'll never tell, for it saved ye from hanging.'

I was silent wondering how much Willy Tyler, never particularly generous with money, had paid the Selbys and where in fact, had he got the money?

'Dinna blame the gentleman too much.' She waited as if expecting me to say something. 'I ken fine it's not my place, but are you – er, is he – ?' she ended awkwardly.

'No, Mrs. Maxwell, he isn't wanting to make an honest woman of me, if that's what you mean.' I remembered his face averted from me throughout his testimony. 'In fact, I don't really expect to ever see him again.'

She gave a deep sigh – of relief, I thought. 'Och, and I'm glad of that, miss. Mind you, a nice enough gentleman in his way, but I dinna hold wi' actors as husbands. And I hear from Sarah that he was awfu' bold, ye ken, wi' all the lassies at Craighall, to say naught o' the ladies who should have known better. I wouldna want ye hurt by marrying a man like that. There's someone better waiting for ye, mark my word, miss.' With that she sprang to her feet. 'You'll have another cup of tea and instruct me what you'll be wanting now you're home again. I've been keeping everything ready –'

Sadly I told her that I had only returned to put Monkshall up for sale. 'The horses must go after all your kind attention to them and you, my dear good friend, I'm afraid, had better begin enquiring for a new position, for I have no means of keeping you here or even of paying at this moment the wages I must be owing you so far.'

'I'm no wanting a single penny, miss – and I'll stay here as long as Monkshall is yours, that I will. Oh, miss –' she wailed and her face crumpled suddenly as if the realisation of what lay ahead had just struck her forcibly. 'It's the only home I've had since my dear goodman died more than twenty years syne.' She dried her eyes on a corner of her pinafore and sighed. 'Aye, miss, you were naught but a wee lass when I first came to the house.'

And for a while after that we indulged ourselves with the nostalgia of the old days, talk of the familiar things that had been our everyday lives, years of plenty with fine summers and good jams and home-made wines to show for them, harvests and Christmases, but we never talked of winters with snow four feet deep, or animals that perished. For such memories belonged somehow with the ultimate disaster that befell Monkshall and we, poor unhappy wretches, were taking refuge in a never-never-land of eternal summer.

After I had consumed a meal large enough to please her, she announced that my room, although dust-sheeted, was prepared. She needed only a little time to draw a bath. The idea was more than welcome but I could not endure the idea of the old woman carting single-handed pail after pail of hot water up two enormous flights of stairs inside Monkshall. She was insistent but so was I and finally we reached a compromise. I would use the tin tub in front of her fire here as the servants did once a week in the old days at Sir Andrew's command.

Still a little scandalised at such an idea, she withdrew to 'see to your room' while I took a leisurely bath before the fire. Then in the robe she had brought down, I followed her quickly across the courtyard and into my bedroom which, with a fire burning, and flowers in a vase, looked exactly as I had remembered it. Before I left the cottage I took all the clothes I had worn and told her to get rid of them. I never again wanted to see anything that suggested my Edinburgh prison.

'But they're too good to burn, miss – your cloak too – you don't mean that to go – and the shoes.'

'I do, I mean everything,' I said firmly. 'Either burn them or give them to some charitable concern.'

As she turned back the bed and stirred the fire to a steady glow, I had a sudden revulsion against sleeping in this great alien house all alone. Bidding her goodnight I wished I had courage to beg for a bed in her cottage. But I knew she would be embarrassed and rather put out at such an idea, it would also mean she would perhaps have to sacrifice her own bed.

33

For all the comfort of familiar surroundings, I slept ill in that dead house, conscious of the shrouded rooms, like ghosts from the past all around me. Each time I awoke I fancied creakings, as though the house stirred restlessly at my presence and that its dreams too, were chilly and frightening.

Towards morning my uneasy attempts at sleep were rewarded by an invasion of Willy Tyler. A strange dream in which we were still in love and he held me in his arms and said: 'The past is over, my darling, my love – it has never been – ' But the voice was not his, nor was the accent which I found difficult to place. And even as I looked at his face it began to change and turn into another I had seen so fleetingly during my trial. The face of the man in the green greatcoat. I awoke sick with dread, with disappointment and fear to find Mrs. Maxwell putting a breakfast tray on the table beside me.

Downstairs, the hall clock chimed twelve. I had slept until midday. 'No, of course you didn't wake me,' I assured Mrs. Maxwell. 'Porridge, how lovely. Now you mustn't spoil me. Yes, it is wonderful to be home again.' And I ate obediently under her watchful eye as I had done often in some childhood malaise. At last satisfied that my appetite was in good order she stirred the dying ashes into a semblance of cheerfulness and gathering together the dishes on to their tray, drew two letters out of her apron pocket.

'These have just arrived. I hope it's good news miss. I wanted to see you eat a good breakfast whatever it is,' she added apologetically as she closed the door behind her.

The first letter was in Willy's hand and Mrs. Maxwell might have recognised it. Remembering the nature of the dream that had awakened me, I opened it with joyous expectation, even some miracle of lost love restored. Perhaps at that moment I even hoped for an offer of marriage after depriving me in public of what little remained of my reputation. Alas, the letter was curt and unloverlike. A brief apology for the embarrassment and discomfort he had caused me, followed by: 'Some day you will no doubt wisely recognise that it is better to live with a broken reputation than a neck broken by the hangman's noose. I leave Edinburgh today but shall continue to wish you well always.'

That was all. A very final curtain, I thought, wondering whether Sir Andrew had been right and all that Willy Tyler had been interested in were my prospects as a possible heiress. 'Wait until I make you penniless' he had cried on that last fatal night, 'Wait, miss, until I cut you out of my will, then we'll see how your fine suitor reacts.'

Somewhere in heaven, I was sure Sir Andrew smiled down grimly. And instead of love for Willy Tyler, I felt only sad for him. I know not why except that he must have been seriously worried to write such a letter at all, worried perhaps that having had my freedom purchased at the cost of a reputation might have encouraged me to feel it necessary to wrap myself around his neck permanently. Indeed I had little right to have received his generous perjury so ill, or to entertain such feelings of fury towards him. Without doubt he had saved my life.

I took up the other letter, in a hand I did not recognise.

'My dear Christina – I have lately heard the news of my cousin Andrew's death with the utmost grief. Knowing of his devotion to you and in view of the unhappy circumstances in which you now find yourself, I am sure he would have wished me to offer you the hospitality of my home for some small period of readjustment. I am much away from home and my wife who is in frail health, would gladly welcome your companionship, especially as our only son is now resident at the university. I am taking the liberty of presuming you will accept my offer and enclosing a first-class rail-ticket to Aberdeen where a carriage will be sent to meet your train. Yours respectfully, Cawdor Faro (Captain).'

The address was 'House of Faro, Egypt Bay, Aberdeenshire.'

I was utterly mystified, so too Mr. Mackintosh, to whom I presented the letter for his advice.

'Faro? Cawdor Faro?' He shook his head. 'I know of no

35

cousin of Sir Andrew's – and certainly I should have remembered such an unusual name. However, as he disclaimed any family – or t'other way round – early in life, it is certainly possible that a cousin Faro exists. His only boast as I recall about his immediate relatives was that both his parents were thirteenth children.'

'Shall I go, as he requests, then?'

'Yes, my dear, I think in your present melancholy circumstances, a change of er, air – might be of considerable benefit to you. Meanwhile, permit me to ensure that Mrs. Maxwell receives her wages regularly and continues to look after Monkshall until your return – '

'And my horses?'

'Precisely.'

3

Railway travel was no new experience for me, even trains moving at frightening speeds like seventy miles per hour brought neither qualms for safety nor any feelings of discomfort. Many females of my acquaintance still feared the consequences upon their health of such gross and unnatural perambulations and as for travelling alone, this was an undertaking in which ladies exercised the greatest caution. Sir Andrew had laughed at their misgivings and described it as 'being subject to the weird and wonderful interpretations of our time. As if our dear Queen had just discovered the evil side of man's nature and that it hadn't existed since time began.'

As for the few men who tried to scrape an acquaintance on the pretext of enquiring after my welfare or regarded me in shocked disapproval, to both categories I was equally indifferent for I had at Sir Andrew's instigation learned early neither to fear nor idolise the opposite sex. He was fond of quoting Catallus on the subject: 'It is not fit that men should be compared with gods.'

I applied myself to contemplation of the countryside, a landscape full of pleasant pastures, flashes of sea, and hills where sheep grazed like the tiny animals I had once owned on a toy farm in childhood. Whatever Sir Andrew would have thought, I felt quite omniscient watching the tiny figures emerging from houses or riding along the roads, humans that belonged to the unreal world beyond the railway line.

I was thoroughly enjoying my journey when we reached the Tay Bridge and were suddenly engulfed in rain and wind.

The bridge seemed to shake alarmingly under the rattling wheels and passengers who happened to be on their feet preparing to leave the train when it reached Dundee Station, were hurled against the windows and had the utmost difficulty in remaining upright, clutching at door handles, window ledges for support. It was all very disagreeable and frightening and I hoped I would never experience a real storm on what seemed a perilously frail structure holding us far above the grey waters.

We left Dundee with rain streaming down the windows and taking refuge behind the newspaper I had purchased at Edinburgh, I read it with sufficient determination to keep at bay the attentions of the portly gentleman who had just entered the compartment and, staring me out of countenance from the seat opposite, remarked with great and earnest frequency upon the inclemency of the weather.

It was as well my interest was absorbed by melancholy news from the Zulu war front and fierce but unbloody skirmishes in Parliament, for the landscape I had hoped to enjoy was soon completely obliterated by sea fog which continued along the coast-line. Thus my first sight of Aberdeen Railway Station on a cold rainy afternoon was far from comforting.

As I left the train, boldness and pleasurable excitement of the unknown had fled and I was subject to all the natural fears of the step I was about to take.

What did I know of Cawdor Faro and his family? Why had I so readily accepted his letter without first making some cautious enquiries? Why had Sir Andrew never mentioned him, if they were so devoted to each other?

I was completely alone in the world. Supposing there were other more sinister motives than compassion, for his desire to lure me under his roof? Supposing for instance that his family were non-existent and I found myself locked in a strange house with a maniac?

Such were my dismal thoughts as I waited under the station

portico where carriages arrived and departed with their occupants. A quarter of an hour passed in speculations growing more and more bizarre. Worst of all, perhaps I had been the victim of some cruel perverted practical joker who thought it all worth the price of a first-class ticket. I would wait no longer. I would be wise and return to Edinburgh, to the safety of Monkshall, at once.

I had reached the ticket office when my arm was grasped by an elderly man, considerably wet and out of breath. Mumbling what I took to be apologies about the conditions of the roads and the weather, he added something about a wheel – all of this in a dialect quite incomprehensible to me. Then seizing my luggage indicated by a nod that I should follow him.

For a wild and giddy moment I wondered if this was 'Cousin Faro'. Red hair and abundant whiskers framed a rosy countenance and extended to ears, hands and neck. Crowning this tumult, a hairy red tartan bonnet. Impolite to smile, but when he introduced himself as Broom, the name seemed not one whit improbable.

Handing me into a handsome brougham waiting outside the station, a moment later we were under way, the horses trotting at a good pace, harnesses jingling as Broom gave them sharp commands in the special language kept for issuing instruction to beasts inclined to waywardness.

Waiting hopefully for a glimpse of Aberdeen, I was rewarded by a grey cheerless vision of deserted streets where the entire populace had apparently taken shelter from the rain. Soon we left the main thoroughfare and headed north along a road of handsome new buildings, between which there were occasional prospects of sea, grey and untempting. Then a flash of sunshine revealed a tantalising backward glimpse of Aberdeen's shining granite spires, turning the town into a sudden mysterious Camelot. Clouds sternly folded in again as if ashamed of this moment's frivolity and in keeping with the weather, I allowed my spirits to droop.

Hungry, depressed and rather chilled I huddled well down into my seat and thrusting aside apprehensions of what might lie at journey's end, I allowed myself some speculation as to the character of this unknown Captain Cawdor Faro. The elegant carriage, its comfortable interior and the aroma of expensive cigars which adhered closely to its upholstery; my mysterious benefactor's notepaper and his generosity, conjured up a prosperous, respected citizen. Imagination painted a stocky sea-captain, bearded, stern but kindly.

Captain Cawdor Faro. The name was whimsical, romantic enough to suggest a young man, polished and elegant and I closed by eyes indulging in a delicious fantasy that my mysterious stranger in the green greatcoat awaited at Faro, instead of this elderly male relative of my late guardian. I sighed, wondering what absurdity lay hidden in my nature, what caprice to make me so cherish the memory of a man I should never see again, whose hair was the colour of the sand at ebb-tide, whose voice I should never hear and whose smile I had never seen, yet somehow knew it would be gentle, tender. Sadly I realised that every mile carried me further from the possibility of ever knowing the answer to the question his eyes had asked. Sensibility said he might well have been a visitor to Edinburgh whom curiosity alone had led to a murder trial.

A tap on the window and Broom's face gazed down. He was pointing with his whip in the direction of a long grey line of sea, a horizon we had been following for some time. Now he slowed down the horses' cracking pace so that I could observe the bay. Sand dunes and wind-blown grass, bleak against a bleaker sky. Cliffs rose from the sea like the mighty hands of a race of departed giants, black, shining, menacing and far below a bright yellow ribbon of sand touched by the flying lace of breakers.

Broom indicated that I open the window. Someone had described this coast of Buchan as the 'cold shoulder of Scotland'. Now I knew why, as for the first time I heard the roar of the sea, the echoing sounds from those bird-haunted cliffs – and then I saw the house. Standing on the edge of barbarous cliffs, even its fine towers were dwarfed by the natural majesty of cliff and sea. I shivered. What must it be like to live cheek by jowl with such a prospect, and conditioned by the elements, what savage traits must the humans who lived in such surroundings develop in order to survive?

Broom urged on the horses and I noticed that the cliffs formed a natural caricature of a sphinx's head. With a shudder I wondered if this cruel unfriendly landscape was Egypt Bay, our destination?

To my vast relief, the carriage swept inland away from the wild shore and through a desolate land of field and heath, whose sole occupants were abandoned crofts or poor thatched cottages; we followed the railway line, a straight track that ran neat and purposefully towards a horizon which presumably contained other marks of civilisation.

A castle came into view. For a delicious moment, I held my breath hoping this was the House of Faro, but nearness brought crumbling ruin, broken turrets and windows long since lifeless. As I gazed wistfully at this relic of a Scotland older than my own time, the horses made a sharp right turn and a glimpse of an ornate modern lodge quickly vanished into the thick of a rhododendron drive. Further twists and turns deposited us before a large modern house, addicted to towers and turrets which the present fashion for domestic building finds quite irresistible. Remembering the ruined sandstone castle, this feeble facsimile of times past had neither conviction, nor grace. Ostentatious and vulgar, the House of Faro suggested the harassed eagerness of a greedy architect, anxious to please a rich client whose wealth was proportionate to his lack of taste.

Broom led the way up the front steps, put down my luggage, gave the doorbell a mighty heave and touching his bonnet said:

'Mrs. Reed will see to ye, nae doubt.'

My thanks for his trouble in meeting me at Aberdeen

Station was received with an embarrassed cough, a non-committal grunt as he marched his horses towards the stables.

With the sound of the doorbell still echoing, I watched him vanish through an archway with an old clock tower, into a small courtyard which presumably housed stables. While I waited I took stock of my surroundings.

From my higher vantage point, I realised this was the building Broom had stopped to point out. Alas, only distance had lent enchantment and considerable drama, although there was evidence of earlier buildings in grass-covered stones. Apart from the luxuriant drive, the house appeared to be gardenless and cropped grass vanished alarmingly in the direction of the cliff-edge. There were no great trees to bring benign illusions of protection, of summer afternoon tea upon the lawn. Seagulls darted screaming against a darkened sky, diving shrilly against shadows, to disappear noisily seaward.

Before me the door remained firmly shut. Feeling that I had waited as long as politeness decreed, I boldly rang the bell again. Nothing happened and I looked around wildly for Broom, with a vision of myself thrown upon his hospitality in the guise of an apparently unwanted and unexpected guest, perched foolishly before his master's door that no one chose to open.

And then I heard it. The sea. I had been too preoccupied with noisy gulls and my own pressing anxieties for it to penetrate until now. The sea. Monotonous, roaring, booming, sighing. Murmuring and threatening, eternal and so persuasive . . .

'Miss Christina Holly?'

With something of a shock I heard my own name. Turning I found the front door had been opened by an elderly female of comfortable bolster proportions who stood wiping floured hands on a large white apron.

'Come away in. The Captain told me to make ye welcome. Leave your luggage there. Broom will see to it. I'm Mistress Reed the housekeeper.' She bobbed the ghost of a curtsey, and led the way across a hall dark in oak panelling and up a fine staircase whose simple elegance had been put out of face by an embellishment of heraldic beasts.

The stairs curved and a kaleidoscope of light turned the wilderness of brown into a magic cavern. The source of this ethereal light was a handsome stained glass window in which warriors wrestled, fought or stared down upon us menacingly, swords drawn. Larger than life they presented a somewhat unnerving prospect.

'Aye, I see ye're admiring the Bruce window,' announced Mrs. Reed. 'I understand it's gey valuable. Came from an old chapel that once stood hereabouts.'

I could well believe it for it seemed that the window had brought with it into the house the atmosphere that prevails in ancient churches which are but briefly aired each Sunday. The reason for this, I discovered, emanated from the wall on our left. Of ancient stone, crumbling in texture. It lacked the breathless modernity so evident in the rest of the house. Rooms whose contents briefly glimpsed through open doors, were heavy draperies, sentimental pictures and the claustrophobic bric-à-brac considered so fashionable. How infinitely I preferred the old-fashioned simplicity of a previous century that still prevailed at Monkshall.

I put out my hand and touched the stone wall. Mrs. Reed, noticing the gesture said: 'It's only right that King Robert himself should look down on us from his window. D'ye know he once had a hunting-lodge on this very spot. All that's left of it is the morning-room downstairs, which I'll show you directly. The new house was built by the Captain's grandfather when Castle Faro – as they called it – became too much of a liability to keep in good repair. Aye, it's a fine handsome building, right enough.'

I thought it as unremarkable within as it was ostentatious without, when at last climbing two small flights of stairs Mrs. Reed opened the door of a pleasant smallish room which overlooked the stables and part of an older courtyard: 'Nae doubt ye'll like a wee rest after your long journey. Ah well, ye'll be comfortable enough here, and I'll send Lizzie up wi' your tea.'

As she talked she straightened the curtains, smoothed out invisible creases on the bedspread and darted a poker ineffectually at a fire which smouldered, smoky and resentful, and I felt, quite unused to this extra burden of heating which had fallen to its unfortunate lot.

'That's that. Ye'll nae doubt be comfortable,' she repeated with some emphasis, as if daring me to deny it. Despite her rather severe manner, she looked a pleasant individual, with a mane of sandy hair growing grey at the temples. As eyebrows and skin were somewhat of the same sandy hue and her plump face covered by a thickish down of hair, she looked for all the world like a large and amiable lion.

Lizzie duly arrived with tea and hot water to wash, and I donned after some indecision my second best gown to meet the Mistress of Faro. Of bronze merino with coffee lace at the neck and wrists it did something to bridge that embarrassing gap between guest and servant in which I found myself.

Mrs. Reed appeared and I followed her downstairs past the Bruce with his drawn sword into the morning-room where I realised the awe and ceremony of her announcement had been well-deserved. We stood in an almost completely circular room more than twenty feet in diameter, with several arched windows on one perimeter.

'This is all that remains of the hunting-tower and the first castle.'

The window embrasures were two feet wide richly covered in pale green velvet. The carpet was the same colour relieved by small bunches of forget-me-nots, turquoise flowers and darker green leaves. Some comfortable but modern chairs which looked worn but agreeable, a few tables, mirrors, a glass-fronted bookcase. Here at least the Faros had been sparing of bric-à-brac and I silently commended them for once, on their good taste.

Behind me an ancient arched fireplace which was left in

44

its original state in the stone wall. Then I saw the reason for the lack of ornamentaion. The portrait –

Somewhere near-at-hand a bell pealed and Mrs. Reed excused herself. The door closed gently behind her and I was confronted with the dominant feature of this magnificent room. The life-size painting in oils of a man in the uniform of a sea-captain. Beard, moustache, and no doubt the luxuriant growth continued beneath the hat slammed squarely down over his eyes as he clutched a spy-glass under his arm.

'Captain Cawdor Faro.' A birthdate more than sixty years earlier and he was so exactly the figure my imagination had painted that the accuracy was both uncanny and amusing. It had obviously been painted in the prime of his life for the man in the picture would be scarcely fifty. Yet, add a few grey hairs to my imagined picture and it was still the Captain to the life. I wondered a little about that stern Calvinist face and what miracles of Christian charity had made him open the doors of his house to me, for I did not doubt for one moment, despite the kindliness of his letter, that this man dominated the House of Faro as effectively as his portrait dominated this room.

I followed the direction of his inimical gaze. He stared out through the windows of the room. I could see nothing but sky to reward him – at first, but when I went for a closer look, I found the reason for the strange green glow about this room, the almost translucent light rooted deeper than the whimsical use of greens and blues.

Below the window, far, far below, was the sea. It rushed at black shiny rocks, retreated and came back first threatening, then caressing. Again retreating, it returned for a further assault. Incredible that cliff or house perched precariously on its edge should have withstood such an onslaught throughout the centuries. I turned suddenly giddy, the effect of pale linenfold panelling, greenish glow and those dark eyes staring beyond me upon that ever-moving sea – for a moment, it was like being on board a ship –

'Captain Cawdor Faro, so we meet at last. I am delighted to make your acquaintance.' I curtseyed deeply to the portrait and laughing out loud, heard an embarrassed cough, which denoted a witness to my absurd behaviour.

Mrs. Reed had returned. 'I'm sorry the mistress can't see you at the moment, but perhaps ye'd like to look over the rest of the house.'

All except one room were over-furnished in a painfully ebullient manner. Mrs. Reed opened handsome double doors to reveal a Sheraton dining-table with silver candlesticks and family portraits staring down from the walls. Here the smell of old leather trapped with the lingering fragrance of cigars, reminded me of the interior of the carriage. Four prim windows hung with elaborate but faded brocade gazed correctly across the lawns toward the drive. The portraits were effective enough decoration but almost every other space was obliterated by stags' heads, claymores, swords and heathery hairy paintings of Highland cattle.

'The family's apartments are approached through the morning-room.' I had vaguely noticed a door near the fireplace.

'It's a grand house, isn't it?' asked Mrs. Reed proudly, closing the last door in our tour of expensively furnished guest rooms, a drawing-room containing a notable Persian carpet and the stately master bedroom with its splendid view of the harbour and the great twisting cliff-line that marks the Buchan coast. However, I suspected that handsome postered bed would never be slept in during Mrs. Faro's lifetime, Like all the upper rooms, the magnificent furniture was already fading, pining from disuse with no one to take pleasure in its comfort.

What I had seen was already in fact a sad museum, for furniture needs to be associated with people, with living, otherwise it becomes a place merely to gather dust, a mouldering unhealthy waste of luxury that only the moths can enjoy, as was evident by the predominant smell of camphor everywhere.

Another door: 'This is Master Garnet's room.' In the nick

of time I stopped myself asking: 'Who?', for I was supposed to know the family. 'Ye haven't seen him for a wee while,' Mrs. Reed continued. 'Ye'll hardly know him, he's so grown up these days – he's at the University going to be an engineer, but of course, ye'll ken that fine.'

The room was neat and tidy, impersonal as any of the guest rooms with no pictures or possessions of the occupant to stamp his personality upon it. At least he did not secretly smoke his father's expensive cigars for there was no lingering fragrance up here.

As we walked downstairs, Mrs. Reed said: 'We don't have many guests now that the mistress is in such poor health. She asks that ye excuse her from receiving ye at the moment. As ye know, she's a very delicate lady, that's why the family apartments are all downstairs.' She accompanied this remark with a curious glance, doubtless thinking the same as myself and wondering into which category I fitted, guest or servant and how I should be treated since neither the Captain nor his wife were present to receive me. 'Perhaps ye'd like to see my kitchen.'

Here at least was one well-used room, with warm fire, delicious smells of new bread. A somehow reassuring room, though a little overdone with framed samplers and texts, all sharply reminding us of the presence of God and related maxims dealing with cleanliness, honesty and associated virtues. Mistaking my contemplation for admiration, Mrs. Reed announced proudly that the samplers were her hobby, she had made them since childhood. She was good with her needle and in better days had often been called upon to sew for the mistress.

Over that cup of tea, I discovered there were other servants than herself, Broom and Lizzie. Stable boys, gardeners, two housemaids and an assistant cook. It seemed a vast household for the maintenance of three persons, a Captain who was frequently at sea, an invalid lady and a young man at university.

'If the Good Lord allows the mistress the blessing of restored health,' said Mrs. Reed in the pious tones of one indicating that Mrs. Faro's health had been withdrawn as a punishment for misdemeanours, then of course, we shall need all the rooms again.' She picked up a half-finished sampler with its assurance that God is Love. She had an alarming predisposition to bring God's name into everything, in the utmost reverence as if he were only a step – and a very slight one – above the Captain in the order of hierarchy. I resolved firmly that if I were to remain in her good graces, I would be well advised to consider my reading matter and put Mr. Darwin and his box of monkeys safely away under lock and key.

The assistant cook, a small girl who looked about twelve years old but was possibly older, staggered in under a load of vegetables which she dumped on the kitchen table, and was promptly rewarded by a lashing of tongue from Mrs. Reed, relating to 'all that dirt on my clean table'. She wasn't considered worthy of introduction and with a frightened bob in my direction scuttled away to the kitchen sink. Mrs. Reed announced intentions of seeing about dinner and taking the hint, I thanked her for the tea and said that I had letters to write, assuring her that I would easily find my way back to my room.

I had no letters to write and if such excuses were to form the pattern of my visit to the House of Faro then I had better speedily acquaint myself with my surroundings. I felt my position acutely. As guest I could remain in my room undisturbed and do what I wished but as companion to an invalid – for such had been the terms of Cawdor Faro's letter – I could obviously seek no such refuge. In that acute limbo of being neither fish nor fowl, I decided to absent myself for a while.

As I suspected there was a path by the side of the house which led dramatically down a sharp flight of steps directly to the harbour, a pleasant picturesque place, dwarfed by the enormous noisy cliffs, with a tiny stretch of sand and a few fishing boats bobbing gently against their moorings on the incoming tide. Nets hung out to dry and the lobster pots awaited the evening departure.

I discovered that the steps divided midway and another flight led in the opposite direction to the harbour into what someone had created as an unlikely garden cut out of the cliff face. I caught a glimpse of rocks and stones and statues and some strange plants. There were also seats where one could perch above the sea if vertigo was not an affliction. These seats were pressed against the cliff overhang which was blackened as if by fire. I wondered who could have ever wanted to light a fire in such an unlikely place. I did not get my answer then as dusk descended and with it the rain, so I hastened back to the house where Mrs. Reed announced that she had been searching for me everywhere.

'I thought perhaps as ye were busy,' she said with a reproachful glance, 'ye might like a tray sent up to your room. This is my night at the Bible class.'

Thanking her for her kindness and feeling relieved that I would not have to spend the remaining hours making conversation, I hurried upstairs where I found I was hungry and also very sleepy. The sea, the different air, I could hardly keep my eyes open. The snow-white bed looked most inviting and without time to laugh at my fears of that morning, or to applaud the good fortune by which I had landed in such comfortable circumstances, I fell heavily asleep.

Towards morning I had a dream so vivid I may perhaps be forgiven in recalling it in detail as it has some slight bearing on my strange history. First I dreamed that I walked in the garden at Monkshall and my stranger from the Edinburgh court came to greet me. He kissed me gently and as we walked through the gardens, plucked a rose which I laid tenderly on a rustic seat. But when I looked up he was gone, and although I searched everywhere it was as if he had vanished into thin air. The agony of that moment was measureless, the finding and losing of him again as real a

49

sorrow then as I was ever to experience in my waking hours.

The dream continued and I was in this bedroom at the House of Faro with dawn breaking over the sea. I opened my eyes and he stood looking down at me, his back to the window. He did not speak but stood motionless regarding me in the dim light. This part of the dream was again so vivid that when I awoke I was sure it was the door closing softly that had disturbed me and that someone had indeed at that moment vacated the room.

When I went downstairs to breakfast I discovered that the commotion of closing doors was real and no doubt accounted for my restless sleep and the accompanying dreams. I found Mrs. Reed very flustered.

'Master Garnet arrived unexpectedly this morning – before six, mind ye,' she added indignantly. 'It seems he's spending the weekend with a party of young friends in Elgin, but dropped in to see his mother. 'I'm afraid he hadn't time to wait and see ye this time, he breakfasted and left again right away.'

Mrs. Reed was clearly put out by this change in routine, far from the agreeably slow pace of life in her kitchen. 'I had ten of them to feed – think of that, *ten* – and without a word of warning, mind you, not a single word. All those young hearty appetites, ye ken, eating us out of house and home.' Her face was flushed and stiff with disapproval and as I insisted on helping her clear away she said darkly: 'And what with the Captain never at home either.'

Plainly she felt put upon that the menfolk of Faro did less than their duty towards a sick woman. 'Especially with Master Garnet going to the university too,' as if engineering gave him some mysterious knowledge of medicine that might be used to advantage.

Two days passed without a summons to Mrs. Faro's bed-side and in that time I had familiarised myself with the geography of the house and solved the mystery of part of my strange dream. Doubtless the young master was a little curious about this new member of the household and had peeped into my room, perhaps even stealthily approached the bed for a better look. As I had then been enveloped in my earlier dream about the garden at Monkshall, his face had become confused with the man in green.

I wondered what the next few days would bring for I found living in this empty manner, isolated from the rest of the world, most tedious. I had been brought up never to waste time and to keep my knowledge up to date by applying myself diligently to the daily local and national newspapers. When I asked Mrs. Reed if newspapers were taken at the house, she seemed surprised and a little shocked: 'Ye'll no' be wanting to read *them* surely?'

When I said this was indeed my intention, she frowned and pursed her lips as if this was some fall from decorous femininity. Then she led the way to a large cupboard in the study where the three newspapers published in Aberdeen were neatly stacked in date order. *The Free Press,* the *Herald* and the *Journal.* I was overjoyed at this discovery.

'Ye may read them as long as ye put them back neatly,' she said sternly. 'The Captain is a great reader and keeps all the back copies. He even takes some of them back to the ship so that he can keep acquainted with what is happening at home.' She seemed a little astonished. 'Are ye sure ye're really wanting to look at them?'

I assured her that I was and saying: 'Well then, I'll leave ye to it,' and she went out looking more surprised than ever at this eccentric behaviour.

It was a warm sunny day and off I marched with my bundle of print. However, I soon discovered that the cliff garden and newspapers did not take readily to each other. Although there seemed to be small circulation of air, they writhed and twisted in my hands. I decided after some twenty minutes that there was a quality – for want of a better name – about this strange garden that I found disturbing. The shadow of the cliff-face even in the early hours of morning was somehow sinister,

51

and I left it with little desire to return. Blackened rocks as if primeval fires had ranged, the winds that blew and teased, threw a chill foreboding over all. It was perhaps the contrast with the gentle sheltered gardens at Monkshall but I felt I would have no wish to linger here even in the heat of full summer with book or parasol, and I found myself clambering hastily down the steep steps looking back occasionally at the stirring marram grass behind me as if it concealed some phantom pursuer.

At last with fast beating heart and a profound sigh of relief I stood on the shore. How ridiculous and fanciful my behaviour, for the cliff garden was barely visible at this angle apart from a rather handsome seat which apparently hung suspended half-way down the rock and looked for all the world like an optical illusion.

No chill winds blew here and the shore was still warm although the tide had long since ebbed. There was a gentle balm in the air, the promise of sunny warm days to come. I walked some distance in either direction along the hard sand, enjoying the exercise and finding childish pleasure in seeing my solitary footprints waiting to welcome me on the return journey. For a little while this tiny world of sea and sand and sky was entirely my own, with its colour fast fading into turquoise and mauves.

As I stood at the tide's edge and looked up at the house perched on the cliff-top, it seemed dreamlike and remote, its modernity an affront to this setting which belonged to the beginning of all time. Suddenly I was loath to return and spend another long evening in my room but when I reached the garden again I found a magic transformation had taken place, the grey rather ugly house had softened, its granite flushed, mellowed, even its towers and turrets were gentle ghosts of an earlier dwelling.

For this was the gloaming, neither night nor day, but a timeless moment of magical indecision and somewhere nearby a blackbird burst into song. In a tremolo of sudden ecstasy, sad and merry at the same time and older than man's frail span on earth, the changeless song caught at very heart and core of life itself. Stopping to listen, I found my footprints in the evening dew on the lawn as though a spectre still pursued me.

Then as I walked under the branch I saw the blackbird clearly, so near he seemed to be singing his passionate longing for me alone and I could see the vibrating feathers on his throat, his yellow beak moving like a mechanical songbird in a cage.

Spellbound in this time for love and lovers, tears pricked my eyes and I closed them, almost believing that when I opened them again I should have found the meaning of paradise, that some strange enchantment might take place or a miracle hoped for might strangely come to pass.

Time moved on, the bird flew off in mid-song with a little startled cry, but still soft-footed I walked in my brave new world, opening the front door I moved as if impelled towards the morning-room to watch the last glimmer of light fade over the sea.

With a sigh, still wrapped in my own world of fantasy, I thought of what I wanted most of all in this world. And opening the door – there he was, waiting for me by the fire.

A man in a green greatcoat, leaning on the mantelpiece, staring into the fire and impatiently kicking a smouldering log.

Slowly, he turned his head, smiling . . .

4

'And who the devil are you?'

The man in green swung round to face me. He sounded alarmed, but that second glance had shattered any illusion that my miracle had happened. This was no witchcraft, no lucky spell murmured in an advantageous moment with the stars in the right ascendancy. Garnet Faro, for such was he, was not like my beloved stranger. And yet –

There was something in that strange ethereal young face, as if the clocks had fallen behind and the fabric of time itself had faltered. For my Edinburgh stranger might in some forgotten youthful image have shared something of the same texture of bone and colouring. The effect of that first glance had been quite uncanny, as if I had turned a corner in enchantment where dream and reality meet and a frail ghost of youth had, Faust-like, regained possession. But the illusion died swiftly and I realised that I had only myself to blame, the victim of self-inflicted torture, tricked by my own desires.

'Well? Cat got your tongue?' demanded the magic youth somewhat imperiously. As he turned up the lamp I knew I had solved another mystery. The dream of a man who had looked down on me as I slept and I felt quite shocked that he should have invaded my bedroom, even from curiosity.

Now I could see him clearly, the face and gentle faun-like beauty with Pan's concealed devilment lurking in bright eyes, coloured in some indeterminate greenish brown, like beech-woods on a sunless day, under pale golden eyebrows that tilted upwards at their corners. A short blunt nose and long upper lip, mouth still curved as a girl's but with a look of petulance and rebellion. Here was one who could sulk – and how he would sulk. The olive tinted bloom of youth, nose not yet as aquiline as passing time would make it, cheekbones still rounded and gently flushed without the telltale hollows that age would carve.

After the initial shock of those bewildering good looks, I wondered if those gentle features, the soft ripe skin, rounded bones would ever weather and fill out into maturity. Perhaps it was mere fancy, this small chill at the heart, but I felt the cold blight, the saddest tinge of despair that this one would neither weather nor change. So had Hamlet looked when Ophelia drowned for his love. So had Romeo sighed when he drank the fatal cup on Juliet's tomb. I shivered and the moment was gone.

He was looking me over candidly, forgetting his manners. 'You gave me quite a turn, you know. I thought you were one of the Egyptians whose murdered spirits haunt us from time to time. Now I see I was mistaken – happily.' He bowed low over my hand. 'Garnet Faro, ma'am – at your service. You must be Miss Holly.'

He held my hand lingering, singing softly under his breath like a cat purring contentedly before the fire. He was not much taller than I. Was he sensitive about this lack of inches for only leanness and that long green coat gave that first impression of height? I discovered later he always wore dark clothes. Suddenly aware that he still clasped my hand he released it with a return to boyish embarrassment. 'At least you are substantial for a ghost.'

'What did you mean about Egyptians?'

'Gipsies, m'dear. They used to camp in the ruined hunting-tower that Bruce built. In winter-time they came – oh, for hundreds of years, and made fires in the cave beside the cliff-garden. One hard winter they were starving and stole a sheep and ate it. The Faro of that day, who must have been an unpleasant sort of chap, had already seduced the Gipsy King's daughter and was eager to be rid of her and her family. So he persuaded the local tenantry, who were also looking for an excuse to get rid of their unwelcome guests, and one night they tumbled the gipsies over the cliff, including the gipsy lass and her baby. When the Faro went down to inspect the carnage next day, she was still alive, lying at the tide's edge with her back broken. Before she died she cursed him and said the gipsies would torment him and his heirs for ever. And from that day, says legend, the cliffs gradually eroded into an image of a woman's head, in her likeness – '

I realised why I had felt discomfort for the cliff-garden with its fire-pocked cave. Perhaps my own gipsy blood was sensitive. I doubted whether I would ever linger there again now that horror from past atrocity had added another dimension to my instinctive revulsion for the place. Behind us the door opened.

'Master Garnet, yer mother has been asking for ye. I didna ken ye were here until I heard the voices,' she added with a reproachful glance in my direction. 'Will ye be staying the night?'

'Yes, I think I will,' said Garnet, eyeing me slowly, 'and what is more, Miss Holly will be dining with me. In here, I think, it's warmer and more comfortable than the dining-room for two.'

'Very good, Master Garnet, I'll see to it.'

'Now if you'll excuse me,' he bowed in my direction, 'we can no doubt carry on our conversation later about the interesting habits of the earlier members of this family.'

Following him out, Mrs. Reed threw a despairing glance of supplication heavenward and I sat down on a window seat and watched, until sea and sky merged into one and Captain Cawdor Faro's shadowy portrait took possession of the room.

*   *   *   *

Later I inspected my meagre wardrobe for an appropriate gown in which to dine with the son of the house. A delicate

57

position for, had I been a servant and he under ten instead of over twenty, the brown merino would have served excellently. Had my host been the Captain and I his guest, the midnight blue moire taffeta would have been perfect. Remembering the sharp look in Garnet's eyes I felt he would be a little insulted at dining with a servant and that I would be more comfortable in the role of guest tonight.

He did not stay long with his mother, for Lizzie had followed me upstairs with hot water and I had made the most rapid of toilettes when Mrs. Reed announced that dinner would be served directly. Perhaps I imagined the faintly disapproving glance at my elegant dress which accompanied her remark.

As I passed by Garnet's room, his door opened. 'Ah, I was coming for you. Shall we proceed?' He offered me his arm and we walked down the stairs in grand style as if he were already master of the house.

It did not take me long to discover that despite his youth, he had acquired considerable charm and, I suspected, some experience with the opposite sex. No gauche manners lurked here, no naïvety and throughout the meal he paid me many pretty compliments on my gown and my appearance, accompanied with such admiring glances that might have turned the heads of impressionable young ladies of his own age.

When I steered the conversation into less personal channels of poetry and literature I found we had a bond of admiration for several modern writers, particularly Sir Walter Scott, Mr. Dickens and Mr. Hardy. By the time Lizzie had cleared the table and mended the fire and we had adjourned to seats by its welcoming blaze, I was applauding my good fortune in having found such an agreeable young man as my first introduction to the Faro family.

Whilst I so thought there was one of those small but rather frequent pauses in conversation in which he attended to the contents of his wine-glass. I had long since declined his offers to replenish my own.

He drank deeply, put down the glass and said: 'I believe you know my father very well.'

'Not very,' I replied truthfully.

'Do you like him?'

'He is a kind man.' Again a truthful answer if evidence of my arrival at the House of Faro was guarantee of generosity.

'Kind,' he echoed, as if such virtue in his father was a somewhat surprising new dimension. 'He likes *you* very much.'

I did not feel this rather probing remark called for comment and in the silence that followed, in which he regarded me steadily and was for the first time that evening I felt, searching for words, I was aware that a subtle change had taken possession of our pleasant evening. For conversation there had been substituted a game of cat-and-mouse in which I did not doubt the role I was destined to play.

'My father's a bastard.' Small wonder he had been searching for words. Now he paused and smiled at me gently but without repentance. 'I've shocked you, haven't I?' He shrugged. 'I don't really care about that, I just wanted you to know that I knew.' Another pause in which I was presumably expected to make some remark, but quite honestly could think of none. 'Are you in love with him?'

'No, I am not.' I stood up. Suddenly the evening had gone sour indeed and I wanted to be quit of this young man, whom excess of wine had deprived of manners and sensibility.

He leaned back in his chair, glass in hand. 'Come along, Miss Holly, let's have the truth for once. I ask you again, are you in love with him?' And without giving me time for further denial he added: 'You realise of course that he's quite besotted with you.'

I sighed. 'I know nothing of the kind and I think it's time I retired.'

'What for?' he jeered. 'Don't tell me you have a busy day ahead of you tomorrow.'

'Whether my day is busy or not can mean little to you. Your

father invited me here with the express reason of being companion to your mother – '

' – And up to now she has not seen fit to receive you,' he interrupted. 'You do, of course, know why she hasn't received you?'

'I do. Because she is indisposed. I hope however there will be an immediate improvement. I'll bid you goodnight.'

He sprang up, swaying a little and blocking my way to the door. 'My apologies, Miss Holly. It isn't often a fellow gets the chance to entertain his father's mistress and I allowed myself to be carried away by the situation.'

'You also allowed yourself to be carried away by imagination, with a little help from the wine – '

'Oh, come now, Miss Holly. Let's not be infantile. Your very reason for being here. A devoted friend of my father's dies, leaves his ward all alone in the world. At the risk of being ungallant, you are hardly anyone's picture of a young and helpless female.'

'That is all you were told?'

'Yes.'

'Then perhaps when you are old enough someone will tell you the entire story.'

'I'm quite old enough to add together two and two – '

'And silly enough to come to the wrong answer.'

'Then supposing you tell me, for I'm more than willing to listen. No, not tomorrow – now, there's no time like the present.' And taking my arm he led me back to the fireside.

'Very well, then. Was the name of my guardian known to you?'

'Sir Andrew Something-or-other. I wasn't particularly interested.'

'Had you not then been reading the newspapers?'

'Newspapers? No, I hardly ever read them. What's that to do with it?'

'A great deal, I'm afraid.' So I told him the story of Sir Andrew's death, my trial for his suspected murder and even

60

how an actor with whom I was acquainted had given false evidence to save my life. At the end I said: 'I hope you realise that had my relationship with your father been the one you suggest, I would have had enough delicacy not to flaunt myself under his roof and take advantage of his invalid wife.'

He looked at me, sober now. 'No, Christina Holly, after what you've told me tonight, dammit, I don't think you would.'

'Then I'm indebted to you for your good opinion. Goodnight, Garnet.' And as I turned to depart I caught the Captain's eyes regarding me rather sardonically, I thought, from his frame.

Garnet reached the door before me. 'Please forgive me. I did have too much wine and I forgot my manners, but please let me explain. My mother means everything in the world to me, my father made sure of that a long time ago. He has never had any use for me, nor I for him. My mother told me at the outset of this last illness several years ago that my father has a woman in Edinburgh. In view of your sudden appearance and your total inability to be passed off as a "young ward", I made a serious mistake which any son could be excused. I cannot bear to see my mother suffer any more – there are other things too painful – I won't go into those now. I can only say I'm sorry and ask you to forgive me. I see that we are not the only ones who have suffered in this life.'

He held out his hand to me. 'Christina, please – let us be friends.'

'Very well, Garnet, friends we shall be.'

But as I left him and went up to my room I was still disturbed by his hatred of his father and decided that it would be wise to stay out of his way.

I slept ill that night and hoped by going down late to breakfast that he would have departed. However, I found him pacing the hall, dressed for riding, and obviously waiting for me.

He watched me come downstairs: 'You look lovely this morning.'

'You're very flattering.'

'It's truth, not flattery. I think you are the most beautiful woman I have ever met. If I were a little older or presumed for a moment that you would take my attentions seriously, I know I should fall in love with you.'

I could think of no reply, the situation was quite farcical and I watched him ride down the drive realising that with the revelations now in my possession, I would be wise to make my excuses and leave immediately, so as not to distress and embarrass Mrs. Faro any further.

Mrs. Reed chose that very moment to announce that the mistress wished to see me. The bedroom was large and gloomy with a postered curtained bed and windows which I suspected were seldom opened. The consequent feeling of suffocation was not helped by a vast array of ornaments, medicine bottles, pill-boxes and toilet articles clustered on every available chair and table.

The occupant of the bed was concealed from me as Mrs. Reed fussed around her patting pillows behind her head, cooing over her with the false heartiness reserved for sick children, the mindless old and, alas, the dying. My suspicions were correct for not even the heavy odours of cologne and flowers could conceal completely the smell of decay, nor could the dimly diffused light from the windows disguise that the woman in the depths of the curtained bed was indeed dying.

She was so shrunken in illness that her poor frail body left hardly an imprint under the smooth outline of bedcovers and when she turned her head it was with the greatest effort. She took my hand, there was a vague attempt at a smile but her eyes searching my face betrayed other strange emotions. Trying to interpret that long glance between us I thought I saw misgivings, even terror in their shadowed depths, which considering her son's revelations were neither unexpected nor surprising.

After my encounter with the portrait of the Captain downstairs, Mrs. Faro was considerably younger than her husband, even depleted by illness, she could not have been much past forty. Her delicate appearance made her look pathetically young, and it was from her Garnet had inherited his ethereal quality, his classic good looks. Without doubt, she was once lovely, the long golden hair although faded and a little unkempt had been her crowning glory. She opened her lips to speak but I could not catch the faint whisper and glancing in despair at Mrs. Reed, she motioned that I move nearer. Mrs. Faro tried to raise herself to speak louder but the effort merely seized the poor woman with a fit of coughing. It seemed incredible that such a volume of noise could issue from that tiny bundle of bones and helplessly I watched as Mrs. Reed ministered to her. Helpless I was indeed for the small claw-like grip of the skeletal hand continued and was quite inescapable without something that might have looked un-happily close to revulsion. So I stood rooted to her side, embarrassed but totally unable to withdraw from the painful scene. At last with her invalid settled, Mrs. Reed became aware of my plight and a moment later I was free with the exhausted lips of the mistress of the house moving gently: 'Come – again – later – '

With the door safely shut behind us, Mrs. Reed gave vent to her pent up emotions and cried noisily into a large white handkerchief. 'Oh the poor love – it won't be long now before the Good Lord takes her from us. And a blessing it will be too, the end of all her sufferings. It's so awful, sometimes I even pray that He won't let her go on – oh dear, oh dear.'

Enquiring for a likely cause of her illness I discovered chronic invalidism for many years since Garnet was born, had led eventually into disease and rapid decline which had accelerated mysteriously during the last few weeks.

'The end won't be long now,' said Mrs. Reed. 'Poor lady.'

'I'm sorry. What of the Captain?'

'Ah, he has many duties – men don't suffer the way we women do. The Captain's a busy man, his ship takes passengers and cargoes here, there and everywhere on the continental trade. He comes and he goes. A man with an invalid wife must make his own life. Besides – ' she hesitated and gave me an oddly embarrassed look, before continuing in a whisper: 'I thought all the family knew how things were.'

I was left to the unhappy conclusion that 'how things were' indicated that the Captain's philanderings were common knowledge in the household. I slept ill that night and had a strange exciting dream about the man in green, who continued to haunt me most effectively since he was the sole memento, the only remaining ghost of my trial. That hideous experience which although it was fading a little from my wakeful hours morbidly refused to be exorcised from the strange labyrinths of the human mind and memory which Sir Andrew loved to discuss. A province now being keenly researched by an Austrian doctor, Sigmund Freud.

Certainly in my own case no one would have been surprised had I carried mental derangement as a result of my harrowing experience. One thing was certain, that I would carry unseen its scars until the end of my days. Nor could the outsider be blamed for thinking this apparent obsession by a complete stranger was part of some damaged fabric of the human mind. There was no other explanation for although he had occupied so brief a period – a matter of hours in my life – his presence haunted me and his face was for ever lurking at the back of my mind. Thus besotted with his image I had even mistaken young Garnet Faro for him.

In terms of witchcraft I was clearly possessed. Neither a romantic woman nor a silly sentimental one, Sir Andrew had long since taught me to scorn such feminine weaknesses and to apply the more scientific explanation such as too-tight lacing or airless rooms, to maladies like the vapours.

Later that day I made a second brief visit to Mrs. Faro. We indulged in a little polite conversation and she requested that when she was stronger I would read to her. When I was about to retire to my room Mrs. Reed met me all smiles and reported happily that my visit seemed to have cheered up the mistress and that I was to look in and see her at any time.

'She seems to have taken a rare fancy to you, Miss Holly. Her actual words were that she would enjoy your society.' And pointing to a bottle on the kitchen table, she addded: 'Master Garnet has this made up in Aberdeen. It's a prescription from one of the professors of medicine and it helps to ease the mistress's pain. I'll put it in the cupboard here, so you know where it is.'

And so began my strange ill-fated friendship with Ruth Faro, in which we played charades like two small girls. For on days when she felt stronger, she would request that I open cabinets and wardrobes and deck myself in a Spanish shawl and mantilla, a coat from China richly embroidered, or a yashmak from North Africa. She would beg me to open boxes of barbaric jewellery which I must then please her by adding to my weird apparel, rows of pearls, strange necklets, rings and bracelets. Then there were seductive perfumes from Paris.

She would lie back against the pillows watching me parade before her with a kind of reluctant admiration, easy to understand. And remarks such as:

'Of course, my husband the Captain chose that one specially with my colouring in mind. No doubt one should have golden hair to do such a garment justice. Really, that one was not made for such a tall thin woman as yourself, one should be dainty, yet well-covered. Yes, yes, my dear, that Moorish costume by all means. You look quite the part, quite heathenish and savage, in fact, in such clothes,' she would add with a polite shudder.

Occasionally Mrs. Reed came in and treated us both like naughty children, scolding but smiling too, and leaving us with clothes spread everywhere. And the sombre room with the sound to the sea would vanish, as these tokens of a more exotic world spilled across the floor and conjured up the

65

strange magic of other shores, shores that managed to exist on the same planet as the chilly world of north-east Scotland in a cold, windy late spring.

Often she talked of Cawdor Faro in tones of warmest cordiality as if anxious to have me understand their devotion to each other. She never referred to him except as 'my husband' or 'the Captain' and sometimes as both. There was a pathetic reverence in her voice, how he would read the newspapers to her and she did miss that. When I told her I would be delighted to do so in his stead, she seemed surprised.

'Won't you be bored, my dear?'

But it was poor Ruth Faro who was bored by wars in Zululand and Afghanistan, by Parliamentary proceedings and Court Circulars and storm-ravaged lands. After twenty years of being an invalid such a world had become utterly alien to her and she wanted only to know what was in the Ladies' Column and what fashions the lady who wrote it, Penelope from London, advised for summer.

Her interest which had flagged at the attempted assassination of the Czar in St. Petersburg and the Durham Miners' strike, or the famine which raged in Morocco where people were devoured by roving bands of hungry dogs, revived considerably at advertisements for the latest novelties in dresses, jackets and French and English millinery.

One day she announced that she did believe she was going to recover from her long malaise at last, perhaps the cure lay in the tonic the Captain had brought from South America or the bottle that Garnet's friend had prepared. It seemed that if she were soon to be up and about again the Captain would expect to see her in some of the clothes he had brought from his voyages.

She asked me to fit on her the mantilla and begged a mirror to see the result. But what she saw reflected would have defeated even the most stout-hearted. A woman even less vain would have wept, for this was the face of death that stared back, ivory, skeletal. She thrust the mirror into my hand, dragged off the mantilla and insisted that I keep it.

'You look like a daughter of Spain,' she said. 'Do you dance too?' The question was so innocently put that I could not imagine she was hinting at my mother's dubious past.

I said, quite truthfully, no, and with a sigh she continued that before her illness she had sometimes gone on short voyages to Europe with the Captain. To Dubrovnik and Piraeus and many others. Strange names, as strange and vivid as the impressions I was forming of Captain Cawdor Faro, as a typical sea-dog, bearded, jovial, full of rich warm life. I had not the slightest doubt that Garnet was right and his lusty father found solace where he could from an ailing wife.

When I went upstairs later to my room, I had a visitor and opened the door to Garnet. After an exchange of some words about the weather, he said: 'I'm indebted to you for the miracle you have brought about in my mother's health. D'you know I haven't seen her so well or happy in years?' He took my hands. 'You're a life-giver, aren't you?'

'I'm not sure what that means.'

'There are life-givers and life-takers. My father comes into the latter category.'

'Are you sure, Garnet, that you are not doing him an injustice? Have you ever thought what it must be like for a man like your father, either away at sea on long voyages or at home married to an invalid wife? Can he really be blamed as long as he doesn't hurt her? Anyway, she obviously adores him and he is very kind to her and brings her back beautiful presents.'

'Adores him – she's terrified of displeasing him. He hates her – and me. And I hate him too.' There was a vindictive return to childhood spite in those added words which made me smile, despite their ferocity.

'I'm sure you don't really.'

He gave me the strangest look and said: 'I shouldn't like to gamble on that if I were you, Christina. I hate him more than anything in the whole world. If by lifting my little finger – so – I could destroy him, then I should do so without a moment's hesitation or remorse. You think that's dreadful, don't you.'

'Yes, I do.'

Suddenly he smiled. 'I didn't come to talk about unpleasant things, but to ask if you'll come to the Opera House in Aberdeen this evening. They're playing *Uncle Tom's Cabin* and I have seats reserved. Before you refuse, let me tell you that my mother agrees it's an excellent idea. Also that you'll be in highly respectable company, two professors' sons, two doctors' daughters – and myself.' He grinned. 'I'll be honest with you. There is a supper party afterwards as Eric's brother is in the cast and the young lady I invited last week has unfortunately suffered a close family bereavement.' He looked at me appealingly. 'I shall feel compelled to refuse if I do not have a partner. Please say you'll come.'

And it seemed a splendid idea to get away for a few hours from this melancholy house where I now spent most of the day at poor Ruth Faro's bedside. I heard myself saying: 'If your mother approves, then I'll be delighted to accompany you.'

Broom drove us into town and stopped to collect another young couple of Garnet's friends from one of the handsome new town houses near Queen's Cross. Unfortunately our departure had been delayed as one of the horses had cast a shoe and the lights had already gone down when we took our places in the theatre with the rest of the party.

I had no programme, no warning and it was impossible to express my horror when I recognised Willy Tyler in the role of Simon Legree. In the interval I learnt that an announcement had been made from the stage that he had taken over the role at very short notice owing to the other actor's illness. There was no way in which I could avoid meeting him or extricate myself from the party afterwards without causing embarrassment and distress to Garnet, who of course was quite oblivious of my situation as I had not informed him of the actor's name in my Edinburgh drama.

I need not have worried. Willy was an excellent actor both on-stage and off; we were introduced, and I congratulated him on his performance while he bowed over my hand as if we had never met before that moment. As usual he was greatly in demand with all the ladies and at the meal which followed in a private room at Cheyne's Royal Restaurant in Market Street, I had the greatest difficulty in getting an opportunity to talk to him alone.

Obviously he recognised my determined approach with some dismay, perhaps fearing a resurgence of my passion for him when he nervously excused himself from his party.

'I have only come to congratulate you on your performance.' As this was the second time I had done so, he perhaps recognised the veiled remark.

'It was a piece of good fortune, as I am between tours and, frankly, I didn't know where next week's rent was coming from. I am sorry for the unfortunate man, of course,' he said, taking my arm and leading me a little away from the others, 'but I hear he will soon recover from his broken collarbone, and meanwhile, thank God, I shall have sustenance until my next tour begins.'

'I wish you well with it, every success. But before I say goodnight, there is one question I wish you would answer for me.'

Again he looked frightened. 'If I can,' he said cautiously.

'I would like to know the identity of my benefactor?'

He frowned. 'Benefactor? I don't think I understand.'

'Yes, Willy, you do. In Edinburgh recently – the person who paid you to tell that story – come now, you know very well what I'm talking about.'

He shook his head. 'I'm sorry, Christina, I can't help you. I never knew his name.'

'He must have communicated with you somewhere. His address will suffice.'

'I don't know that either. He left a note at the theatre saying he wished to interview me about a lucrative role in a play. He was leaving Edinburgh immediately and if I would walk along Princes Street at ten-thirty that evening his carriage would be waiting near Waverley Station. It seemed a little odd but knowing the rivalries that exist in the theatre and the eccentricities of producers – and God dammit, I like a lark – so along I went, and there was the carriage. When I got inside the man told me quickly – what he wanted and handed me a hundred guineas.'

'Ah, then you did meet him. Even if you don't know his name, I'm most anxious to know what he looked like.'

Willy Tyler shook his head. 'I can't tell you much about that, either. It was quite dark inside and a cold night. He was muffled up to the ears with a cap pulled down to his eyebrows. He was a big man, I thought, well set-up and there was one thing I do remember. He was wearing a uniform. I recognised that right enough, it being the same as my uncle's. He was a sea captain – does that help?' he asked.

'It does indeed.'

But as I explained to Willy that Captain Cawdor Faro had also kindly offered me a temporary home with his wife and family here in Aberdeen, I realised I was still not one whit nearer the solution of my mystery. Why, in fact, had he done so? What possible motive was there for this strange generosity?

5

Surprises relating to the enigmatic Captain Faro were still in store. Next morning Mrs. Reed asked me if I would care to go into Aberdeen with Broom and do the shopping as she 'hadna time' and urgent purchases were needed both for the larder and for the mistress.

I discovered Ruth already propped up in bed reading the newspapers when I knocked on her door. I was delighted to see her thus, for even to my astonished eyes, she did appear to be gathering new strength from day to day. Excitedly calling me over to the bedside, she drew my attention to an advertisement:

'Mr. G. F. Sargent's Tour of the North of Scotland, bringing Edgar Wetton's Patent Magnetic Appliances: Cures asthma, croup, incipient consumption, constipation, diarrhoea, dropsy, epilepsy, gout, general debility, langour, lumbago, neuralgia – oh, and dozens more. See for yourself, Christina. Now what do you think of that? I wonder what it's like. "No fee for consultations at 63 Union Street." Oh, if only I were strong enough – '

'At your present rate of recovery, Ruth, I'm sure you won't have the slightest need of Mr. Wetton.'

'Yes, but just the same, I wonder what it's like,' she insisted. Like all chronic invalids, Ruth Faro had long since reached the stage of trying anything no matter how unlikely, as if it were enough to toy with dreams of a cure rather than the reality of the cure itself. 'I have felt so much better since you came. Maybe it's the Captain's tonic. My husband is a great believer in herbs and natural remedies. Sir Andrew would have approved, don't you think?'

71

She looked at me and said gently, 'I hope it doesn't distress you to have his name mentioned, my dear. I've avoided doing so until now, but seeing that we are good friends, there are so many wonderful things my husband has told me about him. He was a great admirer of Sir Andrew's as you well know.'

Putting the newspaper aside she continued in hushed tones. 'In fact, I understand that the Captain discussed my illness with Sir Andrew and it was often the main topic of conversation when he stayed at Monkshall and most anxiously sought Sir Andrew's advice. That coffee cordial over there,' she pointed to one of the many bottles, 'I believe it is doing me so much good at the moment. Now that one was a South American concoction given to Sir Andrew by an old Indian chief. Is that not so?'

My speechless surprise first at Sir Andrew being willing to sit and discuss illness and second at him being party to herbal remedies which had his utmost scorn, was taken for embarrassment by Ruth Faro. She took my hand:

'If this is in any way painful for you, you are to say so and we will talk of other things.'

'No, Ruth, I'd like very much to hear about Sir Andrew and the Captain,' I said with absolute truth.

'You are a wise good girl, Christina.' She shook her head knowingly. 'Ah, the Captain always knew that. He often talked of Monkshall and said how well you looked after him on his visits. He formed a great attachment to you, my dear –' she patted my hand fondly, 'you can well understand how – distressed we both were when we realised how wickedly you had been misjudged. Afterwards I said to the Captain at once: We must have the poor dear child with us. As a matter of fact, my husband never did like Edith, not even as a small girl he told me. And he said only the last time they met – it must have been during the summer a year past when the ship was in Granton for repairs, that there was something he thought, a little sly about her.'

As I listened to this incredible pack of lies I was beginning to consider that not only Edith could be classified as 'a little sly'.

'It was so good of you to have the Captain to stay so often and at such short notice at Monkshall and to give him your particular attention. He is not an easy man to please, but – ' she continued hastily, as if I might get the wrong impression from this remark – 'he is the most kind and considerate of husbands.'

We were interrupted by a tap at the door. 'Ah, here you are, Mrs. Reed, Yes, she's all ready, aren't you, my dear? Here's a list of things I would like from the shops. Now that I am stronger I feel I will be getting up and about shortly. I should like a new shawl, black lace, I think and not too expensive. Grey gloves, size $6\frac{1}{2}$ – and yes, a new parasol for the garden. Oh, I leave that to you, something frilly yet practical too. And some pink flowers for my bonnet – roses would be lovely. And please, Christina, some more of those novelettes we've been reading together. Broom will show you where to find them – '

'The sea-fog's coming in again,' said Mrs. Reed following me downstairs, 'it's no a very grand day for your visit to the town, I'm afraid.'

'I shall enjoy seeing Aberdeen, whatever the weather. And I love looking at shops, besides Mrs. Faro would be so disappointed if I changed my mind.'

'Aye, I ken fine how the poor lady sets her heart on wee treats and surprises. It would be awfu' to disappoint her. Ye've worked such wonders, miss, ye have that. Aye, company was what she most needed. And miracles do happen, we can see that for ourselves if we have faith. The doctors can be wrong. Remember Lazarus,' she warned with total irrelevance and her usual addiction to misquoting the Bible on every occasion. She looked up at the sky as Broom handed me into the brougham. 'Aye, ye'll be lucky if you can see to the other side of Union Street once you get into Aberdeen. Mebbe you should wait a while – '

But I was determined to make my exit for a little while from the House of Faro. I needed time alone to sort out my bewilderment. As the carriage rattled along the road to Aberdeen, I made a determined effort to unravel the mystery of Captain Cawdor Faro who might well be a kind and considerate husband but was also a consummate liar and the possessor of a sturdy imagination, greatly to be envied. To my certain knowledge I had neither met him nor entertained him as a guest at Monkshall.

My first impression from the portrait in the morning-room had been of a lusty virile man, with perhaps a wife in every port to console him for his invalid spouse at home. That a particular one existed in Edinburgh had been confirmed by his son, Garnet.

Although Sir Andrew had been something of a recluse by nature, the Captain's apparent knowledge of the family could have been gleaned on the scantiest acquaintance, from business contacts or mutual membership of gentlemen's clubs in Edinburgh. It was probable that a chance visit to Monkshall on an occasion when I was absent had appealed to him as the perfect cover for his extra-marital activities. The 'cousin-ship' he claimed, I doubted exceedingly, probably a figment of imagination used in the beginning to lull his wife's suspicions.

As for the part Ruth Faro claimed in bringing me to the House of Faro, that could be dismissed as being 'wise after the event'. Having ascertained through Garnet that I was not, in fact, her husband's mistress and seeing me in the pleasing role of companion, she was now deluding herself into pretending that the visit she so feared had in fact, been her own idea.

As Broom briskly directed the horses down King Street, a tell-tale mass of heavy grey mist hung over the city. The spires of St. Nicholas Church and the new Town House hung in the air like pale silver ghosts, but the prevalent gloom did naught to depress my spirits and as the Mercat Cross came

74

into view I was feeling very pleased with myself and my conclusions about Captain Cawdor Faro.

Broom brought the brougham to a halt and poked his head through the window. 'Up yonder's Union Street, a mile of it, all the way to Holburn Junction and straight as a die.' He pointed to an imposing shop across the road. 'Yon's John Esslemont's. Ye'll get Mrs. Reed's tea there.'

I consulted my list and discovered Mrs. Reed's writing rather indecipherable.

'Let's see it. Aye, that's Finest Pekoe Souchong tea – she's awfu' particular aboot it. Dinna let them gi' ye any other kind and dinna pay more than three shillings the pound.' He consulted the list again. 'And what else is there? Uh-hum. Ye'll have to go to the top end of the street ower the Bridge for the mistress's marmalade. Gordon and Smith's the grocer keep John Moir's Seville Orange Marmalade – awfu' fine. Aye, aye, ye'll get these other things there too.'

He thrust the list back into my hand. 'Them other ladies' geegaws, ye may get them up there too, but if no' there's John Falconer's – we'll be driving past it in a minute, corner of Market Street. I'll gie ye a hurl ower the Bridge and ye can mak' yer own way back.'

As this was market day, there was considerable activity of carriages, carts and persons walking and riding. As all were shrouded in fog, the scene took on a rather spectral appearance.

At last Broom helped me alight beside the grocer's shop which was my first call. 'Dinna lose yersel' lass, and dinna let them over-charge ye, d'ye hear now? Ye canna get lost, remember, jest turn round and follow yer nose. Ye'll find me at the Mercat Cross, jest walk back the way we came.' And tut-tutting he said if the day had been clear I would have seen the Castlegate from where we stood, nae bother. 'If ye're wearied, ye can tak' a horse-drawn tram.' I had already noticed these conveyances with some delight. 'They run from Queen's Cross right to the Castlegate. Aye,

aye, ye'll be all right, lass – Union Street's straight as a die.'

An hour later, I had almost completed my purchases and found myself without any difficulty in a charming shopping area in St. Nicholas Street. All that remained were gloves for Ruth. The ones I had turned down originally as not quite right in colour were in fact a better bargain and a better match in the shop near the grocers. A clock unseen chimed three and realising that I still had time in hand before meeting Broom, I set forth through the churchyard of St. Nicholas. Birds sang in the trees among tombstones ancient and modern and a few elderly people sauntered thoughtfully along its paths as if they flirted with the first notions of mortality. Then a small boy emerged gleefully with a runaway hoop, accompanied by a nurse with perambulator and stern admonitions to more decorous behaviour. I walked on, past a seat where two old men argued over their pipes, in a dialect quite incomprehensible. There was nothing of the melancholy churchyard about this thriving meeting-place and I was delighted at so much natural intermingling of life and death.

Almost oblivious to the minor discomfort of blanketing sea-fog combined with the curious dead-fish smell of the sea that permeated everything, I walked happily along Union Street. There was endless novelty in examining each shop window. Besides household goods, oh, the handsome gowns and bonnets, the shoes and elegant capes! How wonderful to be rich, to buy a gown for every occasion and never have to think of the price. I moved on with a sigh, reflecting sadly that I did not even know where my next warm cloak would come from. However, refusing to allow a depressing glimpse of the future to spoil this new experience I decided to walk the full length of the street to enjoy the thrill of taking a horse-drawn tram back to the Mercat Cross in time to meet Broom, who was ostensibly 'awa' doon to the harbour on business for the Captain', but I rather suspected felt a certain need to disport himself with cronies over ale at one of the many inns I had noticed.

At last, clutching parcels and Ruth's gloves, I stopped and bought a small bouquet of flowers for her. The clock chimed again and I decided it was time I caught my conveyance. Alas, this was easier said than done. The mist had thickened and the whole of Union Street was obliterated in heavy mauve gauze. Setting forth to the opposite kerb across such a wide street was like swimming across an unknown sea, with horses and carriages materialising perilously close to one's elbows.

Halfway across, I heard the ominous rattle of wheels and the cabman's warning cry. Instead of dashing ahead, I hesitated, panic-stricken as a terrified rabbit. My lack of decision lead to my undoing. The next thing I knew someone yelling 'Watch out' had seized my arm and losing my balance, I was staggering about the road, with purchases scattered everywhere.

A small crowd, thinking I had been injured and drawn to the commotion, gathered around. Flustered and embarrassed, snatching up my parcels, I assured them I was quite intact and that the cab had not been at fault, it had been entirely my own blame for not looking where I was going.

With the last of my parcels thrust into my arms by a portly gentleman, I looked across at the kerb, *straight into the eyes of my Edinburgh stranger!*

I blinked but he remained. He must have witnessed the whole incident. Turning on his heel he disappeared swiftly into the crowd.

'Wait,' I called. 'Wait, please.' With no idea what I was to say to him when we came face to face I dived after him, thrusting aside the arms and willing hands that seemed intent on delaying me.

'Sure ye're all right, lass?' 'Nae thing broken?'

'No, no. Please let me go.' I could still see his head. He wasn't going to vanish this time. Now that we were both away from the crowd at the kerb, I could see him walking purposefully ahead in the fog. Running swiftly as I could with my burdens I was gaining on him.

'Wait, wait a moment – please.'

At that moment he made a sudden sprint in the direction of a hiring carriage. I had just reached its door when the cabman looked down, said sternly: 'I have a fare, lass. Ye'll need to get another – there's one coming now.'

I watched helpless as they trotted briskly away. The horse-drawn bus arrived at that moment and I struggled aboard, heart still thumping I stared out of the window, staring at every tall fair man with broad shoulders. As Aberdeen seemed full of such gentlemen on that occasion, especially to tantalise me, some of them looked back, rather surprised at the intensity of my ferocious gaze.

Alas, I was much too preoccupied to enjoy the ride I had looked forward to and when I emerged at the Mercat Cross, there was no sign of Broom, but I could hardly believe my good fortune, just a pace or two ahead, a tall fair man in green – I was certain it was he –

I reached his side, put a hand on his arm: 'Excuse me, sir.'

He turned surprised and with dismay I knew I had never seen him before. As I stood apologising, a voice hailed me and there was Broom calling irritably:

'This way, lass, if ye please. Where d'ye think ye're going?' He took my parcels from me and said, giving me a curious look, 'I thocht ye didna ken anyone in Aberdeen.'

'I mistook the gentleman for an Edinburgh friend.'

'Did ye now?' He didn't sound convinced and I wondered if he would report this piece of gossip about that odd 'crater Miss Holly', pursuing strange men in Aberdeen, ye ken. Handing me into the carriage he gave my flowers a look that might have withered lesser blooms. 'There's plenty flowers back in the garden without ye wastin' yer money on the likes of them. They'll no last – '

'They're for Mrs. Faro,' I replied with dignity. 'Besides,

78

even if there are millions of flowers in one's own garden, it is nice to get a present of some specially, isn't it?'

Broom's lack of comprehension of the logic of this statement was a disapproving grunt and I sat back wishing my first visit to Aberdeen which had promised to be so happy had not been marred by another attack of hallucinations.

I wished there was someone I could talk to. For the first time I was truly frightened. For there was something very odd going on in my imagination these days. The vivid dreams, this preoccupation with my Edinburgh stranger – all pointed alarmingly to some mental reaction from all that I had suffered during the trial.

I would have to be careful. Over me for ever hung that most hideous of verdicts 'Not proven'. Did anyone believe I had nothing to do with Sir Andrew's death? Whether or not I administered the fatal dose I was, in my own heart, still guilty. Would anyone sane believe that I was haunted by a man whom I had seen in the courtroom, whose face was not at all remarkable but had nevertheless carved a place for itself in my disordered mind? I must be careful. Incipient madness, incipient madness, was the rhythm the horses trotted out on that journey back to the House of Faro.

*   *   *   *

Ruth was delighted by my flowers and insisted on having them by the bedside. She shed a tear and said that I had been so kind and thoughtful, she felt she owed me her new interest in life.

'My dear, you are so much more than a companion, you are my trusted friend. Please say you'll stay with me.'

'As long as you need me, I'll stay,' I said, patting her hand.

But in the weeks that followed I often wondered about the wisdom of that decision. I wished I knew when the Captain was coming home, for I was most curious to meet him. Once this event took place I think I recognised already that it would be a crisis of mutual embarrassment and worse, on each side. I had much to say to him and afterwards there would be no place for me on his charity or in his house – the die would indeed be cast.

Only my anxiety for Ruth made my present place tolerable. Used to the authority of a busy thoughtful life, I recognised too that I had exchanged one prison cell for another, albeit this one was pleasantly padded with some small measure of velvet. Apart from occasional visits to Aberdeen, where everything was surprisingly normal after my first bitter experience, outdoor activities were restricted to pacing back and forth along the cliffs or walking by the shore, avoiding the cliff-garden, which even before Garnet's revelations, I felt to be a haunted, unhappy place.

As I walked by the tide's edge, I was conscious of a sickness of the spirit, a longing to do do something definite about anchoring a future which drifted aimlessly, insubstantial as a boat on a storm-tossed sea. And as time passed without the Captain's homecoming and I often reflected on his possible reasons for telling his family a pack of lies about Monkshall, and how he had gone to considerable lengths, even the risk of a hideous scandal, to place me under his roof. As I did so his image became more and more sinister, especially as the pieces of his personality gleaned from others at Faro fitted together like a child's puzzle.

His wife was obviously in considerable awe of him and pathetically grateful too, for his continued kindness during her long illness. She indicated clearly wifely devotion and obedience and gave no hint that she hated him or had ever done so, as Garnet maintained. There was also Mrs. Reed, Broom and a staff of servants who respected him but also held him in awe as a stern employer who would not put up with any nonsense from anyone.

Garnet's impeccable hatred never varied. His father was an adulterer, a monster who hated his wife and child and there were the elements of a Greek tragedy lurking on this

Scottish coast, I felt, where son would destroy father if ever chance delivered him into his hands.

At our third meeting when I announced doubts about my future, he said: 'You can always marry me. That will certainly confound the Captain.'

'I would prefer to marry you for other reasons than to spite your father – *if* I were in love with you.'

'Which you are not, of course,' he said, eyeing me sadly.

'Which is probably the reason you asked me.'

He laughed. 'I'm not sure why I asked you, but I think it's a fine idea and I won't be put off with one refusal. I'll keep on asking.'

And so he did, until both proposal and my prompt refusal became a joke. However, even Mrs. Reed hinted that I might be the reason for his more frequent visits home to see his mother, while Ruth quite straight-faced confided to me her hopes that Garnet would not delay too long in finding a suitable wife. 'I would not stand in the way of his choice and,' she added with a sidelong glance in my direction, 'I cannot see any reason why one should disapprove of a wife being slightly older than her husband, especially if she would have a steadying influence upon him.'

Perhaps the age difference was immaterial to Ruth, but I *felt* so much older than Garnet. I had lived through a great deal and he was still an infant in the ways of the world. I was fond of him, he was a pleasing and extremely handsome companion, but far from being in love with him, I felt that behind his façade of charm, a fleeting shadow of the future that cast its blight upon us. As if the enemy's dagger lurked behind the lover's smile, the spoilt child who could still throw toys and break them – and people too – if the mood took him.

I had much to think about on days when the sky brooded darkly and the seabirds' cries sounded like demoniac laughter, which seemed to mock my present predicament and a future nebulous as the sea-fog, that often gathered on the horizon to spoil even the most genial of sunny afternoons. Increasingly, I began to look southwards, shading my eyes against this same glittering sea that washed the coastline near Monkshall. Sentimentally I watched ships voyaging south that would pass within a bird's flight of my home, and I knew I was homesick. On occasions I felt impelled to return to Monkshall immediately and find my own way again in a world I had temporarily lost. Even if this meant relinquishing the identity of Christina Holly and living under an assumed name, I could not escape nor hide away for ever. Doubtless through history other women had faced a like predicament and it was far enough from Edinburgh for the civilised drawing-rooms of society to have been taken over by newer, more titillating scandals. Even Miss Meade's salon at Craighall and her sister Madeline's smaller establishment would long since have been consumed by other lost reputations.

Then one morning, as if my silent prayers had been answered, a letter arrived from Mr. Mackintosh, Sir Andrew's advocate in Edinburgh. As I read its contents, I wondered if behind the mask of impersonal language there remained anything of the old man whom I had only once seen give way to emotion. When clasping my hands after the trial, I saw tears in his eyes. Perhaps he was remembering as I did that he had known me all my life and I had dashed on infant legs across the lawns at Monkshall, when he would pick me up, throw me into the air, and always produce a bag of boiled sweets from his pocket.

Now he was brisk and assured me of his good services at all times. In his businesslike manner of old, the costly upkeep of Monkshall was precisely detailed, with rates and feu duties and a hundred other items which I had always taken for granted. Even empty it apparently had a lusty appetite to be satisfied. Finally Mr. Mackintosh advised an early sale, an expedient move especially as he had already received enquiries from interested private persons. He could not show the house without my permission, of course, but once this was forthcoming, he would immediately put Monkshall on the market. He urged an early decision –

Show the house. I threw down the letter feeling vaguely ill. There was no decision to be made, the answer was all too obvious. Had I wished to keep Monkshall it was too expensive and sentiment without a handsome income would lead to inevitable bankruptcy. But with proceeds of the sale and Mr. Mackintosh's help, I could doubtless purchase a cheaper refuge in Edinburgh.

Show the house. The thought of anyone seeing it at present smote my conscience. Neglect, the stagnation of months, evidence of mice and moth and yellowing shrouds of dust-sheets – surely such a mausoleum would put off many prospective buyers and repulse the sensitive as it had done myself. Its present condition would neither fetch a good price nor secure my future with a modest income.

I remembered that early summer was Monkshall's special season. Beautiful with trees in bud, the gardens echoing from corner to corner with bird-song from dawn to dusk each day. And inside, the rooms fragrant with flowers and fires burning on chilly summer evenings when thunderstorms rolled in fiercely from the North Sea.

And so I made up my mind to return and give it a worthy curtain for the pleasure it had given me all my life. 'Something I will remember with pleasure,' I told Ruth, 'like a mother preparing an only daughter as a bride.'

'Your good sense tells you your effort may be worthwhile financially too. An attractive-looking house will always find a good buyer. Yes, my dear, I think you should go – and very soon.' She smiled sadly. 'Although I shall be sorry to lose you.'

'But only for a little while.'

She patted my hand. 'Of course, of course. However, I shall ask the Captain to call on you when he's next in Granton with the "King Robert", and he can give me a full report on your progress. Besides he will want to say goodbye to the house which has given him so many happy hours of hospitality – '

That, I thought, was one occasion I should hate to miss. It promised to be an entertainment in itself. I assured Ruth I'd return as soon as I could.

She frowned. 'If only the Captain had come home while you were here. There are so many things I wanted urgently to consult him about. For instance – and I'm sure he'll agree with me on this when he sees what a benefit you have been to me – I should like you to accept a salary as my companion. No, my dear, please don't argue, a salary. I insist. The final details must of course be decided by my husband, but I'm sure he will see that we cannot impose on you indefinitely. I know he is going to be delighted at the change in me – why, you have done more with your cheerful presence, your kindness, than all the tonics in the world. And although I shall miss you most sorely, I am quite certain that when you return in a week or two, I shall be up and about again. We will even walk together in the garden. Now what do you think of that?'

When I told Mrs. Reed that I was going back to Monkshall for a while and said that Mrs. Faro was so much better anyway, she looked grave. 'The young master said that we were not to be taken in by appearances, Miss Holly. I'm afraid he doesn't believe in the Good Lord's miracles as I do.' She shook her head sadly. 'He has no real faith, ye ken, although he was brought up to go to the kirk regularly, twice on Sundays, when he was at home.'

After this inevitable preamble on the Lord's behalf, she continued with a sigh: 'He tells me his doctor friends maintain that it's in the nature of the disease that there's an apparent rallying towards – towards the end.' She looked at me tearfully. 'He doesn't think it's possible, not even with the Good Lord's intervention, that the dear lady can last out the summer.'

I found this disquieting, for if Garnet had also furnished Mrs. Reed with such details perhaps I had been wrong to casually accept his apparent gravity about his mother's improvement as a means of keeping me at Faro for his own reasons. I sought refuge in comforting Mrs. Reed: 'Doctors don't always know best, and the will to live is the greatest medicine in the world.'

'And that she has now, the dear soul. And it's all thanks to you, Miss. You've given her hope and made her laugh again. Just like a breath of fresh air in this poor sick house, you've been. Aye, even if you've only given her another two months of happiness, the Lord will bless you – see if He doesn't.'

The following day Ruth bade me a tearful farewell, and I promised to return as soon as a buyer for Monkshall would release me. 'Two or three weeks at most,' I said.

*   *   *   *

How foolish I had been to talk in terms of a couple of weeks I soon discovered when I looked facts – and the condition of Monkshall – squarely in the face. Two months or more would have been more realistic, I thought, posting my first letter to Ruth at the end of my first exhausting week. Mrs. Maxwell had engaged a small army of girls from the village and men to do the garden. We were all hard at work from dawn to dusk, but the house resisted us with unbelievable ferocity, and in those early days we saw little reward for our efforts. The basic scrubbing and cleaning revealed considerable areas of painting were needed to restore the faded glories of scratched doors, sun-blistered windowsills and gloomy kitchen cupboards.

Thus one day dissolved imperceptibly into the next and weeks were measured by vast quantities of soap suds, empty pots of paint and loads of rubbish carried out to the garden bonfire. Apart from frequent letters which I tried to make amusing for my invalid friend I had little spare time to exercise Fortune and Ladybelle, but at least they seemed contented in their field – for a while. And Mrs. Maxwell at the end of a day's hard work to return to her cottage – for a while. Their future disturbed me, and I resolved when a new owner took over that I would do my best to persuade him

85

to take both housekeeper and horses with the rest of the estate.

Originally I had entertained an idea of remaining at the cottage myself, but I soon realised the folly of such an idea. Once Monkshall changed hands I wanted no reminders, nor the hideous restriction of being unable to roam in the beloved house that was once my own. Such would be agonising, like watching a lover with a new mistress, and I knew now as if I saw the path cut clearly ahead that my happiness depended on establishing another world away from Monkshall and indeed from Edinburgh itself.

At least I was heartened to know that there was what Mrs. Reed called 'no lack of money' in Aberdeen's big houses, and the newspapers carried constant advertisements requiring governesses and companions. When that melancholy day arrived on which Ruth Faro no longer needed my services, perhaps I might use my savings from the sale of Monkshall to purchase a dress shop in Aberdeen's handsome Union Street, for I was not unskilled with my needle.

'You need not entertain fears for the future, Miss Christina,' Mr. Mackintosh assured me, looking over the top of his spectacles, for all the world like a wise old owl, 'you will be a woman of property if you will permit me to shrewdly invest the proceeds of the sale.' At the word 'invest' his eyes brightened with the nearest approach to sentiment and animation I had ever seen apart from the day he knew my life was saved. 'And if you will also permit me to keep a lookout for some suitable small property where you can live a genteel existence – I think you will find you might also be able to afford a servant to attend you.'

'Mr. Mackintosh, you are most kind, but do not forget that I have lived a busy useful life since childhood. Sir Andrew saw to that. And the idea of doing nothing but some genteel tapestries with my lifetime devoted to receiving callers and leaving cards is utterly repugnant to me.'

'It is a ladylike pursuit which many less well-off would envy you.'

'Then I wish I had been a boy. I would not have had any of these troubles but would have gone to sea. Why, I could have joined Captain Faro on his ship. Tell me, are you quite sure you don't know him?'

Mr. Mackintosh frowned. 'I have not had the pleasure of meeting him.'

'But I understand he *is* some relation of Sir Andrew's – a close friend. A frequent visitor at Monkshall.'

'That he may well have been, but I do not recall him in the slightest. But to return to your present position. If I may say so, it has long been my opinion that Sir Andrew did you no great service by bringing you up to scorn the given conventions of femininity – '

Such an attitude certainly added an extra complication, I thought with a sigh, gathering up another armful of curtains and covers to wash, as he departed. Perhaps if all else failed I could find a responsible post as housekeeper with the Captain's recommendation, since I gathered at Faro he was a citizen of some repute in Aberdeen. At least I would make a splendid washer-woman.

It seemed unlikely that I would need to change my name or go through life with an assumed identity if I went to live there. Fears that Christina Holly's notoriety had reached that shore were groundless, for looking through the back numbers of Aberdeen's three newspapers stacked neatly on a shelf at the Captain's request, I found only one mention of the trial, dismissed in a small paragraph:

'A verdict of "Not proven" was delivered at the Edinburgh Court yesterday, and the young woman accused of murdering Sir Andrew Howe earlier this year was released on the production of fresh evidence which clearly indicated that the deceased had committed suicide while the balance of his mind was disturbed.'

Perhaps my future lay in a small cottage in Aberdeen where I would take Mrs. Maxwell to live with me. She could have her chickens and I could raise garden vegetables. If such seemed an unexciting prospect then I told myself I had had excitement enough in my life and I was grateful to be alive, whatever the future held. Washing and cleaning with the village girls was the strata of society to which I belonged by heritage. I was happy among industrious working people and nature had not intended me for a cushioned existence of silks, satins and carriages. I had made one important discovery, that I would be completely happy and at ease in the servants' hall, sturdy and well-equipped to face whatever Fate had in store, perhaps with a butler or a coachman as my ultimate matrimonial destiny.

But blue skies and perfect spring-cleaning weather could not go on for ever. Suddenly storms blew in from the sea with heavy and continual rain, which made outside work impossible, and impatiently I had to wait for another fine spell to tackle the enormous washing which had accrued.

At last came blue skies and a temperature that promised an early heatwave. There was only one small difficulty that might have given a more religious woman pause. The day was the Sabbath on which all manual work was forbidden, and I was alone in the house. To even contemplate washing, much less hanging out the results of one's sinful indulgence, was outrageous. Fortunately, the drying green at Monkshall was well-concealed or I might well have been deterred at the shocked faces peering out of carriage windows on their way home from the village church, to which a little earlier I had seen Mrs. Maxwell in Sunday best bonnet and armed with Bible, also take her departure.

Dare I risk it? Should I? I looked at the sky. It was already hot in the sun and the thought of spending a perfect drying day in enforced idleness fuming at inactivity was too great. I was overwhelmed by temptation. I was all alone and who was to see me? Long before the sermon would be at an end I had the satisfaction of seeing lines of sheets and covers drying almost as fast as I pegged them onto the line.

At the last moment I decided to include the clothes I was

wearing – and had been during this last holocaust of cleaning. I quickly cast apron, dress, petticoat into the wash and then added them to the line, luxuriating in this lack of clothing. How wonderful to be clad in only a shift, with bare arms and feet, my hair drawn loosely back.

I was a gipsy again. I had found my rightful niche in this tired old world. And in that moment of revelation I understood for the first time what it was like to be a woman, to lure men, to love to dance under the sun and stars and the devil was only a monster who had invented stays for woman's torment. I lifted my head and sang, adoring the sun for its warmth on face, neck and bosom, on bare legs and grass so cool under my feet as I curled toes into it.

As I sang I abandoned my whole being to the dance, absorbed and mesmerised by some primitive desire, by the sun-worship of my remote ancestors. Thus employed, I hung out the last of the washing.

'Hello?' The greeting was repeated and to my horror as I searched for the source of the voice – a male voice – the sheets before me parted and a face was framed in them. I blinked furiously. But he didn't vanish.

I closed my eyes again praying that he would disappear as passionately as I had hitherto prayed for his appearance. He remained, again I blinked but this was no hallucination, apparently no dream either.

Smiling, he remained obstinately real and I found myself, face-to-blushing-face, staring at long last into the dark eyes of my Edinburgh stranger.

6

Even as I realised the horror of my underclad condition and
that a speedy escape was impossible, he disentangled himself
from the sheet's embrace and reappeared along an avenue of
curtains.

Apart from lacking the green greatcoat, in every other way
this was the man who had sat through my trial. In accord-
ance with the weather he wore a white cambric shirt,
full-sleeved and open at the throat, a silk scarf tied carelessly
about his neck, dark trousers and shining black boots.

'Hello,' he said again. 'Can you help me? My horse has
gone lame.'

Still speechless with shock, I was listening to the incredible
words: 'I don't know how it happened, Chloe's so reliable.
She's been in marvellous fettle, but we were passing the gates
of this place and there was a woman singing somewhere. I
don't know if that was the cause of the trouble, if it was then
she must have bewitched poor Chloe, for the next thing she
was stumbling about and had nearly tipped me off. Ah well,
I noticed you had horses in your field, so perhaps we can do
something for her – '

As he spoke, I blinked several times, but he didn't vanish,
merely stood there tapping the riding crop against his leg,
contemplating my semi-nudity with amused interest but without the slightest embarrassment. That agony he left to me and
my hands flew in horror to the shift which exposed half my
breasts. Damp with perspiration it clung to every curve of
my body, revealing all.

I stifled something between a groan and a shriek of horror
at my predicament and for a moment wondered if I should

91

pretend to be a servant, a deaf-mute and judging by the stunned expression which was almost all I was wearing, he might with luck imagine I was also half-witted.

But even as the idea struck me as a brilliant refuge, he said casually: 'I believe you're selling the house,' making it abundantly clear that he knew he was talking to the mistress of Monkshall.

'Yes, that is – er, yes, I am.' As I stammered I blushed at the fantasy dreams I had had of this man and groaned to to think that in all of them, I had been seductively attired in white tulle, with a rice-straw hat romantically enwreathed with pink roses. Never in my wildest nightmares had I appeared in such disarray. To be clad in only a shift was almost more of an indignity than being stark naked, without perspiring freely and in addition, having a riot of wild black hair falling about one's face, like a raggle-taggle gipsy. My wits had entirely melted away, I was rooted to the spot, my only thought: I can never do anything to change this dreadful first meeting.

'It is such a perfect day, don't you agree,' he said, desperately trying to keep his eyes from wandering below the level of my chin. 'I decided to ride down to the coast, cross-country. It's distinctly fortunate that Chloe went lame near your stable, isn't it?'

From beyond the sheets and curtains a horse neighed, announcing some impatience with the vagaries of humans.

'I do feel there's a note of distinct reproof in that, don't you?' he asked with a chuckle. 'All right, my dear, I'm coming,' he shouted. 'No need to feel neglected,' and bowing, he indicated that I should lead the way.

Pausing only to give my inadequate garment a determined heave down two inches of bare thighs I pointed out the stables and while he led his horse, a fine black mare, thither, I seized the opportunity to rush indoors, snatch up a gown and run a comb through my hair. I was halfway downstairs again when I realised that this was possibly a nightmare from which

92

I still might awaken any moment. Panic-striken I rushed towards the stable, but he was still there.

He looked up from examining his horse to examining my appearance and although I felt it was greatly improved I fancied a gleam of disappointment in his eyes.

I rushed forward patting Chloe's neck. 'She's beautiful.'

'Yes, isn't she? I used to race her until a couple of years ago.'

There was racehorse in every line of her, nothing of the gentleman's county hack about this fine beast. 'Will she be all right?'

'Nothing serious that a small rest won't cure.' He gave her a playful push. 'You're an old fake, that's what you are,' and followed me out of the stable where he looked up at the house. 'You know, this is an amazing coincidence. Only last week I saw Mr. Mackintosh and he promised to arrange a viewing when the house is ready. My name's Neal.'

Vaguely I remembered the name as one Mr. Mackintosh had mentioned.

'Now that I *am* here, I wonder if I could have a quick look round – only if it's convenient, of course. I realise Sunday is hardly the accepted day to ask you, but I would esteem it a favour – '

'Sunday is hardly the accepted day to be found doing a mammoth washing, Mr. Neal, but needs must. I am not quite prepared, for the house has been neglected for some time. There is much work for a woman alone, so I'm afraid I have been reduced to working on Sundays.' And I seemed to hear a ghostly echo of Mrs. Reed's stern reprimand. 'You knew God would punish you for breaking the Sabbath, and indeed He has.'

Mr. Neal was smiling. 'I should not have embarrassed you by calling without warning if circumstances had not led me here, so unexpectedly.'

'If you make unexpected entrances then, sir, you must expect to be surprised.'

'Surprised, yes, but very pleasantly.' He bowed and although his eyes moved over my face gently enough I felt there was a devil's gleam in them, a mockery that spoke more than any words and caused me to blush furiously yet again.

'Now that you are here,' I announced with a primness I did not feel, 'I shall be pleased to show you over the house,' and I marched stiffly towards the front door.

As we progressed from room to room, I was gratified that Monkshall was beginning to assume its grand and opulent airs, even if the same could not be said for its owner. Mr. Neal made approving sounds and while he looked the house over I was similarly employed. Finding him so exactly the embodiment of my fantasies that I could hardly believe the good fortune that had placed him just an arm's length away, as a prospective buyer for Monkshall.

Occasionally he went forward to inspect a window or a chimney piece and I would pinch myself quite painfully, but I was not dreaming. Strange and most inexplicable was that never having heard him speak until now, his voice sounded as it had in dreams.

Older, stronger, taller, with the disciplined body of a man of action, my hallucinations had done him scant justice, for he was in every way much more prepossessing than my pale dream lover. Nearness brought an abundance of small enchantments. The eyes I had imagined as dark were the translucent greenish brown of shaded rockpools by the shore. The high-bridged nose had caught an overdose of sun and a rosy tan took some of the sternness from his face, making it younger, more boyish, with the bleached lock of hair falling over his forehead. There were deep lines from nose to mouth and the smile I had imagined, tender and gentle in such a brooding face was the fault of an asymmetric mouth, which gave an illusion of smiling on only one side of his face. It was this lack of symmetry that added a wistful look of youth, his profile in repose sad and somehow vulnerable.

As well as his voice being strangely familiar, this meeting

94

had been uncannily precognisant in that my dream had associated him with the garden at Monkshall. But alas, I had been
drifting toward him in that wretched inaccessible cloud of
white tulle, perhaps with even an unseen orchestra playing
some sentimental love ballad, bawled by a tenor hidden
among the roses.

Never had wildest dreams suggested our encounter on a
washday, or that I should emerge half-clad from the midst
of the bedlinen and covers, smelling of soapsuds.

'I must congratulate you on keeping the quality of the
eighteenth century intact, Miss Holly, and resisting the present
fashion for bric-à-brac.' He sighed. 'We live in a slovenly age,
where everyone seems to have forgotten the simple lines of
perfection favoured by our grandparents. This mania to cover
every available space with something else is to be deplored.'
He gave a small shudder. 'And to live amid such embellish-
ments, a perfect purgatory.'

I was suddenly glad I wasn't trying to sell Mr. Neal the
house of Faro which seemed the perfect example of monstrous modernity. 'I could not agree more. I have always
preferred the simple classical lines, be it oldfashioned or no.'

When we were back in the hall with our tour over, he stood
biting his lips, frowning. 'Yes, I am most impressed, most
favourably impressed, Miss Holly, When do you intend
vacating the house?'

When would I be vacating Monkshall? And my dream burst
like one of the soap bubbles that I had encountered with
such frequency of late. Why should my heart sink like lead?
This was a chance, polite encounter, that was all. Why should
I have dreams? I could hardly expect to remain as part of
the furniture and fittings of Monkshall, to be sold off with
the carpets and curtains.

'Of course there are final decisions,' he said vaguely.

My heart sank further. Of course, a man buying a house
of this size, a house like Monkshall would undoubtedly be
for a wife and children, many children –

'No doubt,' I heard myself saying, 'you will wish to consult, er – ' I waited politely for him to supply the details, but he continued to frown, ' – to consider it more closely. I can be ready to leave at any time, I have my arrangements made, just as soon as Monkshall is sold, I can go.' A silence lengthened between us. 'After all, one doesn't buy a new house every day.'

He continued to look up the staircase as if envisaging his furniture and his family ascending it. 'As you say, one doesn't buy a house every day. But be assured, Miss Holly, I shall be in touch with Mr. Mackintosh with my offer first thing tomorrow morning. Yes, I like this house enormously. It's exactly what I'm looking for, and if the figure I intend offering is enough – ' and the one he mentioned so casually was considerably more than Mr. Mackintosh had suggested or I had expected. 'If that is enough, then I shall hope in due course to be the new owner of Monkshall.'

As I accompanied him to the front door, he turned smiling: 'And you may also feel happy that it shall be kept just as you remember it. Rest assured, no stags heads, no hideous sentimental paintings shall ever mar its lovely walls, no anti-macassars, whatnots, knick-nacks embellish its corners – '

In the stables, he took another look at Chloe's fetlock and announced: 'Alas, she is certainly unfit to ride immediately.' He straightened up and said: 'Now, the problem is how do I get back to Edinburgh, apart from walking which I am not in a mood to do.'

'There is a railway station half-a-mile away,' I pointed in its general direction, 'down the road there. But I'm not sure about Sunday trains.' I had a flash of inspiration. 'Perhaps you would care to borrow Fortune and I'll look after Chloe until she's fit again.'

'May I? Would you? That's uncommonly kind of you.' He studied me for a moment, then came the sweet smile. 'I'm afraid I can't return her before Thursday, if that's not too much of an imposition.'

I assured him it was not and gathered Fortune from her field where Chloe was introduced to Ladybelle. Mr. Neal switched saddle and bridle and moments later I stood in the drive, empty of all but a new and splendid dream to add to my collection.

My Edinburgh stranger now had a name and substance and was doubtless capable of those romantic pursuits we had shared only in my dreams. Like a person of indifferent digestion but with an obsession for cream buns, I determined to indulge myself.

The euphoria of first meeting carried me in great clouds of fantasy through the next days, with occasional jolts back to reality which included rushing out to the stable, expecting to see not his horse but my Fortune there. And leaning my face thankfully against Chloe's neck, I would whisper to her wishing she could tell me all I wanted to hear about Mr. Neal.

As the day of our meeting approached, my moods fluctuated wildly. There was no reason for this unease, the certainty of tears waiting to be shed and that ultimate bliss was never to be mine. Even my present happiness seemed transient, doomed, nor did I believe in the pretence that such depression was a natural reaction to the end of activity, for little remained inside Monkshall except minor details of its appearance, all the hard work was now needed on my own.

For our meeting, I had already decided on my best gown, more suitable for a ball than receiving a visitor at home, but the summer garden begged for a gauzy cloud of white – if the weather held. I cast many anxious glances at a sky occasionally darkened by clouds. As long as it did not rain, I was quite indifferent whether I froze to death if I looked pretty in the process. Never had I reached such depths of despair over my looks, or lack of them, never stared so fretfully into each passing mirror. From sunburnt face to red hands, coarsened by hard work, I looked a true daughter of Egypt, while Monkshall, ironically had never looked lovelier.

Even the gardens bloomed in splendour as if they put on

97

a special show, a farewell performance. I thought sadly, a picture that I should treasure in memory long after Mr. Neal had returned to the dimension in my life, destiny had intended for him, and I had other more substantial interests to take his place.

On the afternoon before his visit, I was in the garden when a horse and rider appeared on the drive. I discovered Fortune being ridden by a young man, obviously a groom. Touching his cap, he said: 'With Mr. Neal's compliments, ma'am, and can he please have his own marc back?'

'Isn't he coming for her tomorrow?'

The man stared at me, mystified. 'I ken naething about that, ma'am, he told me to collect Chloe as your own beast here seemed to be fretting.'

'She doesn't look as if she's fretting to me,' I said furiously, pushing her affectionate nuzzle away from my neck. She looked fat and well-fed enough. Something must be wrong, there must be a reason for him giving this poor excuse. 'Wait a moment, will you?' Panic-stricken, I rushed into the house for pen and paper and emerging to find Chloe saddled, I said to the groom: 'I have a note for Mr. Neal.'

'Aye.' He nodded.

'Er – I seem to have mislaid his address.'

He put out his hand. 'Dinna worry, I'll deliver it mysel' safe and sound, ma'am. It'll be quicker than mailing it.'

That was not what I wanted. 'He's still at the same address, I take it.'

'Aye, he is that,' was the obstinate reply, hand still outstretched.

I was making a fool of myself, feeling my face reddden. 'My mind has gone absolutely blank for the moment,' I said with a rather false laugh. 'I had better write it down now as there is an enclosure,' I ended lamely.

'He's still at number 64.'

'Yes. 64.' Getting information was like drawing blood from a stone. '64 – ' I repeated, waiting.

'Aye, 64 St. Bernard's Crescent, ye ken. D'ye want me to tak the letter or not, ma'am,' he said a little impatiently.

'Er – no. I think I had best wait until I see him tomorrow.'

'Please yersel' then,' he said indifferently and disappeared down the drive.

*   *   *   *

I awoke early next morning after a disturbed night and a premonition of disaster. Examining my face I decided it was not one of my good days; however, much to Mrs. Maxwell's surprise I appeared in my best gown, explaining that I was expecting people to view the house.

We had already shared amusement at my embarrassing encounter on the Sunday and she had chided me gently as I expected she would: 'Aye, that's sure to happen when you break the Sabbath day,' as if I made a particular habit of saving such arduous washings in order to break a commandment. 'I well remember how Sir Andrew used to say that the ten commandments made sense even for poor ignorant folk, and that if a body worked six days then he needed his rest on the seventh so that he'd be fit again on Monday morn.'

Certainly if I had unleashed divine retribution on my head by chipping rather than breaking the Sabbath, it came deserved or not, for although I lingered by the windows of Monkshall eagerly watching the drive, Mr. Neal did not appear.

In the early evening, sick at heart, I roamed the still sunlit gardens – ironically it had been a perfect day for white tulle and rose-wreathed hat – I thought of that last desperate stroll as a talisman, if I pretended that I no longer expected him, then he would arrive. The gloaming came and passed with all its beauty and sadness, then stars filled the heavens. I made my way to the stables where with Chloe gone, Mr. Neal might never have existed. Totally defeated and on the brink of tears, I retired to bed, and there lay sleepless assuring myself that

99

he had got the day wrong, he would surely come tomorrow, or there would be some communication from him.

Friday passed in false hopes, Saturday in anguish and Sunday in nostalgia, as I relived the week before with all its disasters and its unexpected sweetness. At such-and-such an hour we were walking here, or talking there, and the clock chimed exactly as it did now. Oh, if only I could turn back time and find him saying: 'I'm glad you have kept to classical simplicity' – and 'Rest assured, it shall remain as you remember it'. Now I found I could no longer see his face clearly when I closed my eyes. It was as if I had worn out his image with constant recollection. Last week, alas, I thought I had learned it bone and flesh, like the lines of a map or a beloved landscape, or the words of a poem, now when I tried to conjure it up, the vision came blurred, wavering and indistinct.

Sometimes I stirred myself to anger with reproaches that this was not the behaviour of a courteous well-bred gentleman. Surely he could have sent some message of explanation. Then saner thoughts asked: 'Why should he bother? He was only a prospective buyer, perhaps he changed his mind, or his wife pouted and said she was well pleased with St. Bernard's Crescent and why on earth did he desire to bury himself – and her too, away from Edinburgh society in the depths of the country? And what would the children do?' And maybe those unseen children clamouring around him had complained too. For judging his age as forty, his growing family might well have future prospects of university for the boys and parties and suitable marriages for the girls. I could almost hear Mrs. Neal demanding:

'How can these ends be furthered, pray, by sojourn away at the back of beyond? And how will I get staff?'

Perhaps he was a man who liked peace at any price – though his appearance suggested otherwise – and their arguments had swayed him. If this was so, little wonder he had not come on the appointed date, for he would surely be embarrassed after causing me to hope that he was intending to buy Monkshall.

Besides such rational explanations, imagination busily painted other eventualities, too hideous to be allowed any other than a fleeting glimpse. A sudden illness, a serious accident, the victim of a robber's murderous assault. Useless to tell myself that some mystique existed between us by which if he died, I must know instinctively. The man was a stranger, a cipher, although he now possessed a name and address.

It was that piece of information finally decided me upon a daring course of action.

'I intend going to the Edinburgh shops today,' I announced to Mrs. Maxwell when she brought up my breakfast. 'I shall need some summer clothes when I return to Aberdeen,' and casually picking up the newspaper I added: 'I see Charles Jenner are having a sale. "A depression in Trade. Special Cheap Good." See? And there's McLaren in the High Street advertising washing print dresses for two-and-fourpence each. I wonder if you would like to accompany me?'

Mrs. Maxwell was delighted and although I had no particular wish for company, the plan I had in mind would appear more convincing had I a chaperone.

We joined the Edinburgh coach at the gates of Monkshall and after a journey thick with gloomy speculation from Mrs. Maxwell about 'trashy goods' passed off as sales bargains, we were duly deposited at the junction of the High Street and the Bridges. Despite Mrs. Maxwell's warnings, we both found bargains in plenty and well satisfied with our purchases, walked to Charles Jenner's, where I purchased a pretty lace cap for Ruth Faro.

Summoning a hiring carriage, I gave Mr. Mackintosh's address in Queen Street. 'While we are heading in the general direction,' I said to Mrs. Maxwell, as if in afterthought, 'I noticed some properties for sale in the newspaper this morning, in the vicinity of Stockbridge and Dean Village.'

'Perhaps we should go there first, then Mr. Mackintosh can look into it, if there's anything that pleases ye.'

Ten minutes later we were driving along St. Bernard's Crescent.

Number 58, 60, 62 – and there on the frosted ground-floor window of number 64 in gold letters large enough to satisfy my curiosity: 'R. Neal and Nephew, Exporters'.

To my delight number 66 was empty, a For Sale notice in its window. Asking the coachman to stop I invited Mrs. Maxwell to follow me and rang the bell which echoed hollowly through the obviously empty house.

'Come along, we'll try at this office next-door. Perhaps they might have some information about the former tenants.'

With fast-beating heart I ascended the steps. Another moment and I should be face-to-face with Mr. Neal. Alas, there was no reply to our summons. I tried the door-handle but it too was locked.

'It must be their half-day,' said Mrs Maxwell. 'It's none of my business but d'ye really want a house this size? Wouldna' ye be better off in a wee cottage somewhere?'

'Perhaps you're right,' I said returning to the carriage, with a wistful glance at curtained windows on the first floor, bringing realisation that I was at last looking on the hallowed dwelling of my Edinburgh stranger.

In Queen Street, Mr. Mackintosh made us welcome and listened with sympathy to my anxieties about selling the house. 'An anxious time, my dear, an anxious time. However, we have had one offer – ' he paused took out a letter and said: 'It's from a Mr. Neal. A quite substantial offer – most heartening. However, we may yet do even better. Here are the names of three more interested parties who will be looking in on you – '

'This Mr. Neal, do you know him?'

'I have had business dealings with him through the years.' He laughed. 'Ah, my dear, you need not worry. The business is sound, steady as a rock, if that's what's worrying you. Long established, thoroughly reputable Edinburgh firm.'

'Has this Mr. Neal a family?' I could hear my heart hammering.

'I know nothing of his personal affairs, but I would imagine it highly probable. A single gentleman would hardly require an establishment as large as Monkshall.'

During the following days, two couples and one middle-aged gentleman arrived to inspect Monkshall. All were apparently as favourably impressed and made much the same comments as Mr. Neal had done. All promised to get in touch with Mr. Mackintosh and make their offers without delay.

Seeing the last of the prospective buyers depart, I sat down wearily, drained of all energy. After Mr. Mackintosh's revelations, my tortured speculations about Mr. Neal's advent into my life were neither destined nor dramatic. Monkshall was a famous Scottish house, Mr. Neal had wealth and some small interest in architecture.

Why should I blame the man for curiosity no greater than my own in investigating his home in St. Bernard's Crescent? Attributing to him motives and emotions of which he was innocently aware, I was furious that he was not returning a passion which existed only in my imagination, without either his knowledge of the slightest encouragement from him.

The final days for offers dawned and I decided upon an immediate return to Aberdeen where Ruth Faro needed me if no one else did. The die would be cast by now, the lucky buyer notified and the final clearing of the house, after a few treasures had been stored, could be safely left in the capable hands of Mrs. Maxwell and Mr. Mackintosh.

Yes, I would travel north immediately and let my arrival be a pleasant surprise for Ruth. The railway from Aberdeen to Inverness had, I was told, a halt conveniently placed within walking distance of the House of Faro. Having made my decision and feeling a great deal more settled and contented than I had done for some considerable time past, I went out to gather the first roses that bloomed on a sheltered bush in the garden. The sun shone, I felt happy, assured that I was beginning a new phase of my life, the past already retreating. At last I was behaving like a strong sensible woman –

'Hello.'

I looked up from the roses and there he was coming down the path towards me. 'Hello, Miss Holly. Good afternoon to you. When I found you absent from the house, your house-keeper told me where to look for you.' He smiled. It was a surprise, I had forgotten the warm tender smile that quite transformed his face. 'I said I would announce myself,' and with a bow. 'Here I am.'

It was then I wondered why I had not heard him approach, for the drive was clearly visible and the sound of a horse cantering should also logically have been clearly audible. And a cold shiver went down my spine, for it was rather uncanny, as if he were a demon lover who had provokingly decided to materialise just when I had resolved to cast him from my mind for ever. Then as if he read my thoughts, he said:

'I took a short cut – across the fields there. I left Chloe to graze with your horses,' and pointing with his riding crop, 'do you ever take that way to the Edinburgh road? It cut quite two miles off my journey, a little rough for walking but splendid riding country.'

Without waiting for a reply, perhaps a little embarrassed that his unexpected arrival had offended me in some way, he continued hastily: 'You must be wondering what had become of me. My business, as I told you, takes me away from Edinburgh for varying periods, and I am afraid there was an unexpected crisis which delayed my return. I have been over the border in Newcastle for the past three days. I must apologise that you did not receive my note which I left on Chloe's stall to be delivered to you when Fortune was returned. Alas, some accident befell it and only yesterday the groom discovered it behind a drinking-trough.'

'You owe me no apology, sir,' I lied gallantly, 'I have not been in the least anxious, especially when Fortune was returned, for that seemed the main reason for your journey.'

'I hope I did not inconvenience you.'

'Not in the least. I have been busy with prospective buyers, and as I was confined to the house by their impending arrivals I scarce noticed your non-arrival.'

As I talked his eyes moved across my face, my neck, in that disconcerting manner that seemed neither ill-bred nor curious, but was as gentle as a lover's caress. It left me chagrined with vanity that I was not wearing something more rewarding and romantic than a serviceable striped grey cotton gown that made me look more than ever like servant than mistress of the house.

'Actually there was no need for me to return,' again that engaging crooked smile, 'for I decided on Sunday evening and Mr. Mackintosh informed me only this morning that my offer had been accepted and that I am the new owner of Monkshall if you can bear to part with it.'

'My congratulations, sir, may I wish you every happiness of it.'

He bowed. 'It seems a happy enough place.' There was a small pause. 'However, even relieved of a mere duty call to return your horse and with not the slightest excuse to call on you, I should still wish to do so to thank you for receiving me so kindly – and may I add, so advantageously, last Sunday.'

'I am glad it worked out well for you, and that Monkshall will have someone who will keep it in the tradition to which it has long been accustomed.'

'I shall endeavour to do so. And now that matters are settled, I wonder if you would do me the honour of dining with me this evening – to seal our bargain – and, of course, there are many small matters still to be settled – '

'I would be delighted,' I said, my voice, I thought, just a

105

fraction over-eager, already leaping ahead with the vision – at last – of the white tulle gown.

'Very well, I shall collect you at, say, seven-thirty?'

Then something very odd occurred as we walked together through the early roses. In exactly the same manner as had been the substance of my dream at Faro, he plucked a rose, sniffed it approvingly and presented it to me with a small bow. 'Roses to the fair, I believe. But I firmly maintain that it should be roses to the dark. Red roses so obviously belong to young ladies with long black tresses.'

I took the rose but was careful to retain it, against the pattern of that oddly similar dream, for then I had laid it down and looked up to find him gone. He showed no signs of dematerialising this time and chatted about house and garden until we reached the field where Chloe cropped patiently waiting for him.

'Until tonight, then. A'voir, Miss Holly.'

I watched him canter down the drive, still clutching the rose in my hand. All that meeting had lacked from the dream was the kiss. Perhaps that too would come later, with candlelight and wine. I could at least hope it would.

'He seems quite a nice gentleman,' said Mrs. Maxwell doubtfully, and when I told her he was the new owner of the house, she added a chorus of approval, in case I shared her misgivings.

'Would you like to work for him, do you think? Shall I ask him to keep you here at Monkshall? He didn't mention having domestics of his own.'

'Oh, would you, miss? It will be wonderful not to have to leave my little cottage after all.'

'Very well, I am to dine with him this evening, and I shall mention it.'

'Oh, he is not married, then?' she asked with a gleam of interest.

'He hasn't spoken of a wife.' I looked at her sternly. 'It hasn't occurred to me one way or the other. This is merely

106

a sealing of our bargain, a business meeting, with all the small details of selling the house to discuss.'

'Of course. Doubtless there will be a wife and family. I can't imagine a bachelor wanting an establishment of this size, can you?' she said contentedly, obviously concerned with her own future at Monkshall.

As I prepared to meet Mr. Neal I realised gloomily that Mrs. Maxwell was probably right and that somewhere in the course of dessert he would casually mention his wife and try to interest me in his children, expanding on their many talents, their charms and virtues. Trying hard not to hate the absent Neal family and realising that tonight was all I would ever have to remember of their lord and master, I began my toilette early, and, taking great care, concluded that I had made every move possible to improve what little looks I had.

When I took my place at his side in the carriage, I resolved that whatever happened in the future this meal at the Cafe Royal would be an evening to remember. Strange, in retrospect all I can remember clearly is the dress I wore and that he looked magnificent in evening dress with a short black cape lined with red satin.

At the table he took my hands and subjected me to an intense scrutiny. He smiled and I waited for the inevitable compliment, but he merely shook his head and wagged an admonishing finger at me.

'White, my dear Miss Holly, is the colour for blondes. It is too insipid for you – like your namesake, your colour is holly red, the scarlet of Christmas berries.' Eyeing me narrowly, he added: 'I should like to see you, not in pale pastels, but in red, emerald, midnight blue – the vivid living colours of roses, bright grass and evening skies. No, no, pale shades hardly do you justice – although you look very lovely,' he added somewhat as a conventional afterthought.

I remember little of the actual meal either, as I foolishly pretended a head for wine which I do not in fact possess.

107

The finer details of river-caught salmon, roast duckling, peaches in brandy, merged imperceptibly into coffee and Mr. Neal lighting up his first cigar.

We must have talked to each other, but memory eludes me with any details, during that long meal. Afterwards, when perhaps the addition of solid food to wine had made my mind more receptive, I remember that he asked if he might call me Christina and asked that I should call him by his first name: Rob. Rob Neal. I felt disappointed, it was such an ordinary name for such an extraordinary man.

One thing emerges clearly through the haze of wine and food. We shared a similar interest in literature and had an argument about the Misses Bronte.

'Does it not astound you, Christina, that women living such sheltered lives could produce such works of passion as Cathy's doomed love for Heathcliffe and the smouldering temptation of Mr. Rochester?'

I remember banging my fists on the table and saying: 'Do all women have to be milksops, are they so different in their emotions to men? Sometimes one would think that men regarded women as members of an inferior species.'

He gripped my hands across the table and said softly: 'Well, well, we have a very passionate young lady here I see, and well within the traditions of Miss Emily Bronte.' He smiled. ' "If we prick them do they not bleed – " '

'Your quotation is misplaced, sir. As I remember it refers to Shylock and not to Portia.'

'Touché,' his eyes narrowed slightly. 'But then I am not a learned man, and I see we have the makings of a blue-stocking. Yes, a prospective member of Women's Rights, if we don't watch out – another glass of wine?'

It was either anger or further indulgence that soon after-wards provoked a distressing bout of hiccups. Distressing and unladylike, it refused in the face of known remedies to depart, so we departed instead taking it, alas, with us, the undignified companion of our drive back to Monkshall.

As the horses trotted over North Bridge I found I was suddenly cold. Despite the early June evening there was a mist rolling in from the sea that reminded me, like a cold hand at the heart, of the House of Faro and that I had not heard from Ruth for several weeks.

'You're shivering,' said Rob. 'There – ' and he wrapped his cape about the two of us so that it was another shared intimacy that I would remember. 'My poor child, hiccups and shivers – what next? Here, rest your head on my shoulder.'

This I was nothing loath to do, and with a contented sigh I thought that for all the money in the world I would not have missed a single moment of those miles back to Monkshall. As for sleeping – which I must have done – for at one point I dreamed I was in the carriage with Broom driving to Faro and I opened my eyes to find Rob smoking a cigar. From my nest in the region of his collarbone I could hear his heart beating above the sound of the horses' hooves.

He looked down at me. 'Does this disturb you?'

'Not at all. I like the smell of cigars, especially those ones . . . I know that fragrance.'

'Do you now? Discerning girl.' He looked at it thoughtfully. 'These are a very fashionable brand just now among wealthy gentlemen. They are the best that money can buy – imported from Holland.'

'I know a sea-captain who smokes them.'

He smiled. 'Then you must compliment him on his good taste. Now, if you hadn't liked my cigar, I was going to pretend that smoke was an excellent remedy for hiccups.' His arm tightened around my shoulders. 'You go back to sleep – '

'I wasn't sleeping, just resting my eyes,' I said guiltily, and sat up straight.

'Of course you were, my dear girl. Why didn't you warn me that wine made you sleepy? Now, you go back to sleep and I promise to smoke quietly so as not to disturb you. We'll soon have you safely home.'

109

'I'm quite wide awake,' I protested furious with myself for missing all those minutes of his society. How I would rue that wasted time, and it seemed that only moments later he was handing me out of the carriage and into the front door where Mrs. Maxwell, surprisingly white-capped and aproned at this hour was waiting for me, as if she did so every night.

She bobbed a curtsey and with a ghost of a wink in my direction, disappeared. Rob turned to the coachman: 'Wait for me at the end of the drive, if you please.' And when the man departed he took my hands and I stammered my thanks for a 'most pleasant evening'.

'Really, Christina, is that all the thanks I deserve?' And without waiting for a reply he leaned down and his face was blotted out as he kissed my lips. A brief warm pressure, a gentle kiss, but I needed no other miracle that evening. 'You do not object, I trust. You look very kissable and see, over there, a moon almost full above the trees. It does seem a pity to waste such a romantic setting. You're very silent?' he said anxiously, regardless of the fact that he had not given me much opportunity to voice an opinion.

I regarded him, hands primly folded. 'I don't mind at all.' I wished he would talk less and kiss me again.

'It was intended as a compliment. You must make allowance for mere masculinity, too. A moon and a pretty girl do strange things to a romantic man.'

Strange, but I would not have thought his nature romantic, but even too shrewd for such a confession of weakness. I heard myself saying boldly: 'It was very pleasant to be kissed at the end of such a lovely evening.'

His head shot upwards. 'Then may I call on you again?' he asked sharply. 'Would tomorrow afternoon, say, be too soon?'

'That would be delightful. Perhaps you would come to tea and Mrs. Maxwell will make us some of her delicious scones,' I added hastily, assuring him that I would be adequately chaperoned.

He bowed. 'I can hardly wait for such a treat. Perhaps we might also find a moment from this splendid banquet on Mrs. Maxwell's delicious scones to talk about my future tenancy of Monkshall? There are doubtless many questions which occur to me on which you might offer advice – '

'Advice,' he said next day, buttering his fourth scone. 'That's what I need. To know how a man single-handed is to run a place the size of Monkshall, in the absence of a Mrs. Neal – '

I restrained a smile of sheer delight, although I had told myself many times during the last eighteen hours that his behaviour was that of a single man.

'In the absence of a Mrs. Neal, I wonder if your Mrs. Maxwell could be persuaded to stay on as housekeeper – she is certainly an excellent cook, too, I would imagine from the spread before us.'

'I'm sure your suggestion would be most welcome to her. She is very anxious to find another position and would be most reluctant to leave her cottage.'

'That's settled then. As I have mentioned to you, my export business takes me to the continent with some frequency, and for a little while I shall not be a great deal in residence at Monkshall.'

As I poured him another cup of tea, he looked very thoughtful. 'It's like this, Christina, I am going to need someone reliable to staff Monkshall for me – I have a house in Edinburgh from which I also run my business, but a man on his own needs little more than a *pied à terre*. I wonder if it would be an imposition to ask you if I might employ your services to engage staff, look after things and also my Chloe. Take on anyone you imagine necessary for the smooth running of the place. Would you do that?'

'I would be delighted,' I said eagerly.

'Then you will in fact be chatelaine of Monkshall until I return to live here permanently.'

After we had discussed various details of how many servants, and some financial arrangements, names of reliable traders, and so forth, Mr. Neal looked at his watch and announced that it was time he took his leave.

We walked out to the field where Chloe awaited him cropping contentedly. 'It promises to be a beautiful evening,' he said, sniffing the air. 'Yes, it's good to be alive on a day like this.'

All around us from every corner of the garden bird-song echoed and we were held in the fragrance of flowers and the soft murmur of trees. I knew sadness then, that I was going to miss Monkshall more than I ever imagined.

As if he read my thoughts he said: 'You must of course, continue to think of Monkshall as your home, consider it in no way different from before. For when I return it will be to ask you to be my wife.'

7

In the silence between us, I heard night birds calling across the garden, the ominous chime of the hall-clock.

His wife. Surely I had misheard? 'Your wife?'

'Yes, that is what I said,' he replied casually. 'Surely my proposal can hardly be a great surprise to you?'

'I never dreamed – '

'Then you are lamentably unobservant, my dear. I was considerably drawn to you when I first saw you in Edinburgh – in less happy circumstances than these – and since the Sunday when I discovered you in considerable but charming disarray, I must confess your image has never been absent from my thoughts. I decided that very day I was going to have Monkshall – and you.' He sighed. 'I can never remember being more love-lorn – '

'Love-lorn?'

His jaw tightened, he took my shoulders and gave them a little shake. 'My dearest, there is no need to repeat every word I say. You have the assurance of my devotion and there are, I hope, more worthwhile ways of expressing your own sentiments.'

Now he had my hands, examining them. Oh, not my hands, I thought, so red and ugly. 'For I have flattered myself,' he continued softly, 'that this feeling was shared, that there was even – some response?'

He leaned forward, kissed me and broke away angrily, hands on hips. I saw the flash of temper, poorly restrained, the sudden thrust of jaw with all the symptoms of stubborn pride I had somehow suspected lurked behind that strong face.

A temper he would hold in check like a wild dog on a chain – and God help all those who passed by during its unleashing.

His tone was icy, far from lover-like. 'Come – you can do better – '

'Better?'

'Yes, my dear, better than that. You know what I'm saying – I expect to be kissed with a little more warmth. Like this – Let's try again.' When he released me, it seemed a long time later. 'As I suspected, there are fires for us both to light and the resulting flame should be well worth having.' He lifted my chin and smiled. I had forgotten that he could also be gentle and tender too, and I smiled back, thrusting out of my mind completely that here was a man I could fear as well as love.

'That's better, my darling, much better,' he said. 'Remember we are two people in love and love is not only romantic novelettes and roses but a powerful emotion of sex, which I assure you can be a happy and rewarding experience. I am not without some acquaintance with such matters, but then you would hardly expect me to be innocent at forty-two, would you?'

And without waiting for my reply, he continued : 'I believe you have fires to kindle and awaken. That was my impression the first day I ever saw you that you were somehow different from the pretty chocolate-box girls who were the lamentable experience of my youth. I thought I detected smouldering passion, a sensuous woman in the making – ' He paused. 'I trust I am not embarrassing you?'

'Of course not.'

'Is that all you can say? "Of course not?" '

I wanted to say that I had never expected a proposal of marriage to be explained in such direct terms but his face was cold and withdrawn, his voice bored and for a moment he was as inaccessible as the stranger I had first seen.

'My dear Christina, right at the beginning of our relationship, let's get one matter settled between us. I should hate

114

you to consider that being loved by me in every sense is somehow degrading, either a fate worse than death, or something a married woman must patiently submit to, as her duty for the sake of begetting children.'

'I don't think of marriage that way, I assure you.' And standing on tip-toe I kissed his mouth, which was disconcerting because he remained statue-like in my embrace, his eyes wide open.

'As we seem to have moderate understanding on this score, perhaps when I kiss you in future,' his eyes flashed, 'I will not receive coy comments about enjoying being kissed at the end of a pleasant evening.' There was nothing tender about our next embrace and I touched my bruised mouth. 'That wasn't very pleasant – or was it?' Again he was smiling. 'But at least it informs you very clearly of my intentions, of a man who will be in every way your lord and master. I will not have any simpering modern miss as my wife – do you understand? Now, will you have me?'

'Of course I will.'

'Do you love me?'

'I love you.' I put my arms around his neck. Love was a poor word to say all I felt at that moment. Adoration, worship, overwhelming desire, anything he asked of me he could have –

'Will you then wait for me, without question, without doubt?'

There was a small chill growing at my heart. Fear again, fear of losing him, fear of something about this man that terrified me because I did not quite understand it, because it was beyond my limited knowledge and experience. It was as if I stood on the edge of a dark precipice.

'There will be inevitable delays and frustrations before the wedding day can be set, because of the nature of my export business, which as I've told you carries me abroad a good deal. But whatever happens, you must believe and trust me, believe that whatever strange requests I make, I am completely and absolutely yours. You and no one else has my entire devotion. You are the woman I love with all my heart to the exclusion of the whole world. You are the woman I have chosen to be my wife.'

With that speech which seemed so odd then and stranger in the light of what was to follow, he took his departure. I watched him go calmly, with no indication of a heart and aching body that longed to whisper: 'Stay.'

He looked in almost every day while waiting rather impatiently, for the ship which was to take him to Hamburg to attend to his export business. He indicated that departure at this time was tiresome but inevitable, and he wished to get these details settled so that nothing would interrupt our honeymoon. On his visits he neither stayed long nor attempted to revive any of the passion he had aroused on the evening he had proposed.

Sometimes sitting chastely side by side considering various items needing attention within and outside Monkshall, such as redecoration and renovations he considered necessary, also lists of estimated expenditure on servants and supplies, I felt I was indeed chatelaine and this was the role he had intended for me all along. On such occasions with the briefest greeting and a cold calculation of the number of roses needed for autumn planting, it seemed incredible that we were destined to share intimacies of bed and board and that some day I should bear his children.

Curiously enough, the prospect of marriage had destroyed the easy friendship that had once existed so briefly, and instead of becoming better acquainted with each successive day I felt we were less so. Cold, remote, he retreated again into being the stranger I had once dreamed about. The discovery that I was marrying a very wealthy man did nothing to quell the awe in which I was tending to regard him.

One sunny afternoon as we walked in the garden he looked better pleased than he had of late, and said: 'Things are moving at last. Well, Christina, next time we meet it will be for our wedding. What do you think of that? Why do you frown, surely you will be here when I return?' he asked smiling.

'Of course I will.'

'Then why are you so preoccupied? Come, does the idea of marrying me no longer seem as attractive as it did two weeks ago?'

'Now you are being silly.' The sun turned his hair into molten gold, too pale and vulnerable for the stern face with its deep tan. He took my hands and his smile was radiant. 'Forgive me, I cannot bear that you should think of anything else when I am here – I'm even a little jealous of those roses you prune so diligently,' he said in mock anger. 'Rest assured, I shall not stay long away from you. I shall be back at Monkshall before you realise I've gone and you may occupy the time prudently by buying your trousseau – yes, and an elegant wedding gown.'

'I thought I might make my own, Rob.'

'Make you own? Whatever for? My dear girl, I can well afford to indulge you in the extravagance of a Paris model. You might try Meldrum and Allan, or Charles Jenner.'

'That would be lovely, but you see, I have always known exactly how I want to look as a bride, with a white dress and veil – '

'A little rustic, my darling, for my taste. And please, not white. It does not become you – far too insipid. You know my views – '

'But it's traditional, Rob.'

'Traditional – what do we care for traditions? What rubbish.' He paused, then added gently: 'Tell me, are you planning to have a large wedding with a hundred guests?'

'I have no one to invite, bar a few acquaintances.'

'And I was an only surviving son, with few relatives and none in this area. Like yourself, I have acquaintances but none that I care for so deeply as to wish them to witness and share the most cherished moment of my whole life.' He

117

smiled at me tenderly, clasped my hand and kissed it. 'All I wish for is a simple quiet ceremony to be got over as quickly as possible, so that we may begin the rest of our lives together. For such an occasion some elegant dress with a fashionable bonnet will do admirably.'

Stopping, he narrowed his eyes, surveyed me speculatively. 'Crimson, deep green, deep blue, would be my choices.'

'As you wish, Rob,' I said meekly, but my disappointment showed, for he put an arm around my shoulders and resting his cheek against my hair said:

'As you wish, indeed. For heaven's sake, wear white if you've set your heart on it. I'm not being parsimonious, we can well afford it.'

'No, you are quite right. It is being very stupid to spend money on a white bridal gown which will lie and yellow in a trunk just to please the sentimental whim of a few hours.'

He nodded approvingly. 'I'm glad the decision comes from your lips. Have you any close friend you wish to attend you?'

I thought for a moment. 'Alas, I have only Mrs. Maxwell.'

'No one of your own age?'

'No one but Ruth.'

'Ruth?'

'Yes, Ruth Faro. She lives in Aberdeen, but she's an invalid and this journey south would be quite beyond her.'

'Then you had better arrange matters with Mrs. Maxwell. Meantime, I will arrange for the banns to be posted in my parish of Edinburgh.' He looked at his watch. 'You will be here when I return – promise?' he whispered.

'There is only one thing that could take me away. This friend Ruth I mentioned. She befriended me and I was her companion until Monkshall's sale recalled me. She is gravely ill – and perhaps dying. If she needs me at any time, then I must go to her.'

'By all means, do so, if your duties from Monkshall and

118

myself can spare you.' He paused. 'Incidentally, I think it might be kinder if she is indeed as gravely ill as you imagine to refrain from telling her that you are shortly to be married. I have encountered similar situations and at such a time, the thought of losing one whose affection she relies on might have an injurious finality. An innocent evasion would be kinder than a truth which might cause needless distress and shatter the short happiness of a lamentably brief future.'

'What then would you suggest I tell her?'

'I would suggest you allow her to think of your circumstances as unchanged and that you will be returning to her as companion once your affairs here are settled. However, you must please yourself, I am only offering an opinion.'

His opinion had the ring of sensible advice, especially as I had already made up my mind not to distress Ruth with the idea that my forthcoming marriage would take me for ever away from her. I was, however, agreeably surprised at Rob expressing my own sentiments and felt it augured well to our amicable settlement of some of the greater problems that marriage must inevitably bring.

*　　*　　*　　*

I was preparing to retire that night when I heard the front door open and close. Expecting Mrs. Maxwell, I was considerably surprised when Rob appeared.

'I hope I didn't alarm you. I let myself in with my key.'

He looked shaken and dishevelled, his clothes dusty, muddied and his face bleeding down one cheek.

'Rob, what on earth has happened? Are you badly hurt? Oh, my dear – '

Turning his back on me he helped himself from the wine decanter on the sideboard. 'It's nothing. I was visiting friends for dinner, not far from here. On the return journey my carriage lost a wheel, that's all,' he said irritably. 'I decided not to delay further waiting for the coachman to get help from my friends' grooms, but merely walk across the fields, borrow Fortune and ride back to Edinburgh.'

I brought water from the kitchen and bathed his face. He winced somewhat but I felt the whiteness about his tight-set mouth was more with suppressed fury than with pain.

'There now, is that better? Shall I make you some tea?'

He indicated his glass. 'No, no, the wine is excellent. I must go now.'

'How on earth did it happen? Where do these friends live – would I know them?'

'It was an accident, I don't know how it happened. One moment I was in the carriage, the next in the ditch. No, of course you wouldn't know the friends I was visiting? Why should you?' he demanded irritably. Then smiling as if the idea amused him, 'I can assure you, they would hardly have achieved Sir Andrew's visiting list.' And his face darkened for a moment as if he were back with them and the topics at that imaginary dinner-table had been far from pleasant. Aware of me again he stroked my hair, said gently: 'I must go now.'

I thought for a fleeting moment I saw a question mirrored in his eyes. I knew instinctively what the question was for the house was silent, empty, we were quite alone and I had no doubt that my answer would be: 'Stay –'. The next instant he had released me and was hurrying out of the front door. While he saddled up Fortune, we talked like polite strangers about the weather, and if it would rain before he reached Edinburgh.

Ready to leave, he turned, grasped me close in his arms. He looked down into my face, very intent and still and I saw the question again shape in his eyes and then swiftly die.

'I may not see you for several weeks, but letters can be forwarded from St. Bernard's Crescent. Whatever happens,' he added, his voice harsh now, 'remember I love you.'

Remember I love you. How often I was to seek solace in the echo of those words that anchored my miracle, my fantasy love into a world of reality. He had said 'Remember I love you,' and closing my eyes I would think of his face. Sometimes when I did so, I tried not to remember other things, such as his cold and suppressed violence on that last night, far deeper than an accident to his carriage merited. I kept on seeing his bruised countenance and how when I kissed him lightly, I smelt wine on his breath. That did not alarm me, for it fitted perfectly his account of dining with friends. But when I drew closer to bathe his damaged face, I was assailed by a heavier fragrance than cigars, a musky heady perfume a seductive woman might employ. And again, taking his evening cape to brush, the white dust on his shoulder might have been powder from a woman's face and those three neat parallel lines down his face inflicted by an angry woman's fingernails.

One thing was certain, whoever or whatever had caused the damage to his person and his composure, had been of fiendish character, and imagination substituted another image for the mere misfortune of a carriage accident and reluctantly labelled that image 'female'. As I attended to the flowers, I told myself I was being disloyal and distrustful, behaving like a jealous woman. The perfume had been expensive hair pomade, the white powder dust, the scratches from some bush, but still the image of a violent and infuriated woman remained and the ingredients of disaster churned together in my mind, ingredients worthy of the cauldron stirred by Macbeth's three witches.

Next day, however, all such queries were wiped from my thoughts when Mrs. Maxwell appeared with a letter. 'Mr. Mackintosh's clerk drove over with this specially and said it was to be delivered to you immediately with a message to expect Mr. Mackintosh himself later today, if you are at home to receive him.'

Inside the envelope was a letter in Ruth Faro's somewhat shaky hand: 'My dear Christina – What has happened to you? Have you forgotten your poor friend so quickly? I have written but you never reply. Perhaps you have left Monkshall, so I am sending this to Mr. Mackintosh whom you mentioned to me. I pray that he will know where you are. Please come to me, my dear friend, as soon as you can. I think I am dying.'

As I packed in readiness to leave Monkshall, Mr. Mackintosh arrived. 'I have but a moment, I am on my way to dine with a client. You must forgive me for opening the lady's letter, I had no idea it was addressed to you as your name had been omitted from the outside.' He held up a small bundle of letters and placed them on the table. 'I think you will find that these are from the same lady.'

'But how –?'

'The explanation is simple. Mr. Neal, like many gentlemen who travel abroad a great deal, leaves such trivialities as the re-direction of mail in the hands of his clerk, who had told the post office that *all* mail addressed to Monkshall was to be re-directed to St. Bernard's Crescent until his master's return. Presumably he then forgot to inform Mr. Neal that there were also letters to the previous occupant – yourself. Such was the explanation I received from the unhappy clerk. A silly mistake but most inconvenient.' And he snapped his jaws shut in the manner of a man who would like to say a lot more but feels restraint is more discreet.

As I accompanied him to the door, I said I hoped he would come to my wedding and he promised to do so, if he were in Edinburgh at the time.

'I imagine you will have a great many friends,' he replied to my earnest hope that he would be present. When I told him that it would be a very small wedding, he looked surprised: 'I imagined that Mr. Neal, whose mother came from these parts, would have many friends.'

'How long have you known him?' The words were out before I realised how shocking, how prying they sounded.

Mr. Mackintosh looked at me, thought for a moment and said: 'For about ten years. He took over the export business when his uncle, the late Robert Neal died. As I told you when he purchased Monkshall, our dealings have been purely business.' Again he frowned and gave the appearance of a man

122

who has something to say and cannot quite find the words, then bidding me adieu he climbed into his carriage and departed down the drive.

I cannot adequately describe my feelings of distress when I read Ruth's letters, which changed markedly from cheerfulness to deepest gloom. The first letters were full of the Captain's homecoming and his delight at his wife's improvement in health. The description of many new things he had brought her including some more of her very special coffee cordial, which was doing her so much good. There were mentions too of Garnet and rather coyly, how much he was missing 'our dear good friend and longing for her return'.

Then as I opened subsequent letters, a note of weariness and despair crept in, even her handwriting deteriorated noticeably. I resolved to leave on the next train to Aberdeen and there are no words to describe my forebodings as I prepared for that departure.

The thought of leaving Monkshall was like physical agony, I was sure that by deserting the scene of my happiness I was stepping out of an enchanted world, and when I returned it would be to find it vanished without trace and I should have lost my love for ever. I would re-read Ruth's letters and wish I were at Faro and a moment later, wish I was going anywhere but there.

Perhaps such over-dramatisation can be forgiven me as I was missing Rob greatly, longing to be safely re-united with him and much of the journey I would have enjoyed in less heart-rending circumstances passed by unregarded, as I wrestled with my problems, real and imagined.

Almost oblivious of the sunlight on the distant sea, of birdsong in hedgerow and tree, and distant seagulls on the clifftop crying a welcome back to the House of Faro, I left the train and five minutes later the familiar drive came in sight. It was only then that I guessed how greatly Christina Holly had changed since her first visit. Despite inner misgivings and forebodings, I had nevertheless acquired a certain poise and security, thanks to Rob and his love for me. I was no longer uncertain of myself, but cherished, adored. When I entered this daunting house I would this time be in command of the situation, remembering that I came as guest and in a little while I would be mistress of Monkshall, an ancient house of grace and charm.

As a wealthy business man's wife, I would be able to meet the intimidating Captain Cawdor Faro on an equal and cordial footing, however, even cushioned by a comfortable well-off existence, I was unlikely ever to forget that I had known the other side of the coin. Danger, fear, and heavy manual work as great as any humble servant girl. I trusted such sobering thoughts would keep from me the unwholesome superiority with which many women of the middle and professional classes continued to regard servants, as less than the ground on which they walked, a kind of inferior breed of human being. At least my husband-to-be shared my enlightened views and in many ways he had much in common with Sir Andrew. I often thought the two men would have enjoyed each other's company for they both had similar approaches to life. In fact, had I searched the world for a man to take my late guardian's place, I could have done no better than Rob Neal.

When Mrs. Reed opened the door, she greeted me like an old friend: "Oh, Miss Holly dear, ye're back – ye're back at last.'

Quickly I asked after Mrs. Faro and she shook her head, her eyes filled with tears. 'She's had one of her awfu' bouts, ye ken, when it seemed impossible that the Good Lord was not going to snatch her away from us. Ah, but now that ye're here, ye'll hae' her back to health and strength, jest as ye did afore. An' ye'll be meeting the Captain too,' she added in an awed voice. 'Aye, he keeps everything and everybody busy, so he does – '

But my curiosity about the Captain was no longer particularly great. I felt I had his measure, and as I took off my bonnet and she prattled on raising her eyes heavenward, that she had this to do and that, and this meal specially and that, 'for the Captain is very particular when he's at home, and disna let us forget that he's the master – '

'Tell me about Mrs. Faro,' I said, for although I was amused by Mrs. Reed's descriptions of the Captain, he sounded an irritating man, something of a tyrant and a ogre and I had to admit, I felt similar tremors in my own heart at being subjected to his patronage and condescension, not forgetting the actuality of that piercing scrutiny of the portrait downstairs which I felt typified the master of Faro.

'I'll tak ye tae her the now,' said Mrs. Reed and as we walked along the corridor she whispered, 'The Captain isna in at the minute, ye ken, he rode off to Aberdeen this morning, he'll be so surprised to see ye, won't he just?'

Ruth's greeting was loving but extremely tearful, clinging to my hand pathetically as if she feared I would fly from her side again immediately. When I explained that I would have been here long since but for the infuriating mix-up about forwarding her letters to me, by the new owner of Monkshall, she didn't appear to be listening.

'It doesn't matter, my dear, it doesn't matter in the slightest. You're here and that's all I care about. Why, I knew in my heart that something had happened and you would never have deserted your poor friend. You'll stay with me this time, Christina, promise. Promise you won't leave me.'

Reluctant to make a promise I must break, I realised with a sense of horror that this was a promise I would sadly be able to keep. Her time of remission was over and death was very near. If it was possible, she was more skeletal than ever and it seemed incredible that a mere frail set of fleshless bones could continue to stay alive. There was another kind of horror this time for she was beginning to suffer most dreadfully in the agonies that marked the final stages of her disease. When I sat down to read at her request, the beads of sweat were on her face and she moved constantly this way and that, moaning, weeping. Her despair would have torn the hardest heart.

Mrs. Reed came in with tea and said as we adjourned from the bedside: 'Someone should do something, ye ken – it's cruel and wicked too that the poor dear lady who has never harmed anyone should suffer like this. Even the strongest pills the doctor gives her are no longer deadening the awfu' pain – '

She was terribly thirsty and between us we helped her sit up and drink several cups of tea. The temperature did not appear to worry her and she gulped down scalding hot tea, like a dying man in a sandy desert, her eyes bright, tortured. I prayed at that moment that she would be released from a burden of life she could no longer support. If there was a God in heaven and He could not save her, then let Him slay her – but quickly, not this hideous lingering end.

Brushing away the tears, I pretended to adjust the pillows. Mrs. Reed departed with her tray and somewhere in the house I heard a door bang and a man's footsteps which seemed to go in the direction of the morning-room.

Ruth heard them, she looked alert, touched her hair in a pathetic gesture, struggled to sit up against her pillows. 'Oh, Christina, that will be the Captain home again. Oh dear, I do not like him to see me so out of sorts. Indeed, I don't, it distresses him so dreadfully. Help me, my dear, help me, before he comes – '

I wrapped a pretty shawl around her shoulders. 'He brought me this from Brussels, isn't it beautiful? I was hoping I could wear it in the garden when you returned. But I shall be careful with it, I must have something nice to wear when we walk in the sun together. Oh, Christina, you have no idea how I long to go out and listen to the sea and watch it again. But now that you're back, you'll take me there, dear, won't you? Just as soon as I'm stronger.'

I promised and tidied her hair, plumped up her pillows and together we looked towards the door for the Captain's arrival. Just then a bell rang resounding through the house and a moment later Mrs. Reed appeared.

'It's the Captain, ma'am.'

'Tell him to come in, Mrs. Reed. I'm quite awake and we are both waiting to receive him.'

'He sends his respects, ma'am, and says he'll be with you directly, but he would like a word with the young lady first.'

Ruth patted my hand. 'Away you go then, Christina dear, don't keep him waiting. You know the way. Mrs. Reed, you stay here please and tidy away some of these bottles – oh, and that table there. You know how he hates clutter and untidiness.' She looked at me. 'Off you go, my dear,' and in a whisper she added: 'He's a difficult man but not unkind, please be patient with him, for my sake, dear. Oh, I do hope that you two will like each other.'

I hoped so too, but with reservations. I owed him gratitude for he had taken pity on me after my trial and offered the hospitality of his house. But now as I walked towards the morning-room, the first image of a kind benefactor was overshadowed by the unfortunate impression I had gained by living in this house. The large aggressively strong man who looked out of his portrait, something of a bully, imperious with his demands, impatient with his ailing wife, antagonising his son, a tyrant to the servants and, I suspected, a liar and an adulterer –

Warm and secure in my new-found happiness, as I waited outside the door, I thought tenderly how lucky I was to love a man like Rob Neal. Called upon to 'Enter', I did so, without any fear at all.

Instead of the portrait dominating the room, it was almost overwhelmed by the Captain's physical presence. A tall man in naval uniform, he rested one elbow on the mantelpiece. His back turned insolently towards me, he was smoking a cigar, its fragrance sweetly familiar as the voice demanding:

'And what the devil d'you think you're doing here?'

He swung round and I stared horrified into the angry face of Rob Neal.

8

'I asked what the devil are you doing here?' Captain Faro walked swiftly past and closing the door leaned calmly against it. 'And before you faint or scream, my dear girl, and you look ready to do both, please think of the consequences – '

The room was filled with strange sounds. Far below the window the sea boomed eerily preparing for a storm. There was another storm raging closer at hand, it originated from my own heart as it's dreams curled up and one by one died.

'I have no intention of fainting or screaming, but at least I think I am entitled to some explanation.' The voice sounded cold and far-off, the words indifferent, uncaring. Where did they belong in the same world I had created with the once beloved man before me? Yet he remained tauntingly the same, eyes green-brown and mocking, the gentle ironic smile, the fair hair falling in disorder over his forehead. Now I realised I had been right, my senses had not deceived me entirely for there was some faint resemblance to Garnet, for whom I had once mistaken him, at dusk in this very room.

I indicated the majestic portrait of the dark-bearded man wearing the same uniform. 'If you are Captain Faro, then who is he?'

'Cawdor Faro, my father. He died two years ago. My name, my dear,' he added with a weary sigh, 'is Robin Neal Cawdor Faro. My father, alas, no longer considered two names quite enough for any one man to bear and I'm afraid I cared little for his choice of Robin beyond childhood. The export business in Edinburgh belonged to the Neals, my mother's family, and I found it convenient, as there had always been a Neal in charge – to save confusion – '

'I see,' I interrupted impatiently.

'You don't see in the slightest, however, you will let me finish. There are matters which must be cleared between us.'

'There are indeed.'

He stood back eyeing me narrowly. 'You're taking it very well, I must say. Far better than I had ever hoped when I discovered that despite all my attempts to withhold communications between my wife and yourself, you had arrived here –'

'So you admit it – you deliberately intercepted her letters to Monkshall. Oh, how could you do such a thing to her? How could you be capable of such cruelty to a poor dying woman?'

'I had our future, yours and mine, to think about. I merely wanted to spare you unhappiness. Cruelty,' he added softly, 'you don't know the meaning of the word yet.' And suddenly he was at my side, I was close in his arms.

'My darling, don't you understand, I wanted to spare you all this. Why do you think I deceived you? Because I loved you, because I wanted – oh my God, how I wanted – to come to you as a free man. Some day you were bound to find out that I was the Captain, your benefactor, but by then I hoped to have bound you to me, to have your love so completely that we were one heart, one soul, one body.'

For a moment he held me at arms length. 'And now I see by your poor stricken face, so pale and yet so strong too, that I have done everything wrong. Forgive me, Christina, forgive me for not being able to bear the thought of losing you.' His lips touched mine. 'No, you won't kiss me – damn you – damn you! I love you and you love me, but you stand there like a prim cold little statue, because in spite of all your emancipation, your grand theories, you have been betrayed. Betrayed by a married man. Oh, it's laughable after the way we talked to each other – come here.' He kissed me without love, with only a passion that bruised my lips and left my heart untouched.

'Now tell me that you love me and want me.'

I turned away from the fierceness of his eyes. 'I don't know,

130

Rob, what I want – except to die, or wake up and find I'm dreaming. Perhaps both – '

'Tell me you love me – ' Impatiently he seized my wrist, dragging it to his heart, twisting it cruelly, but I felt no pain then, until I saw the bruise next day. 'Tell me – ,' he demanded.

'All right, if you want me to.'

'Yes, I want you to. Tell me.'

'I'm telling you that I love you.'

He bowed. 'I'm charmed, especially by that damn-you-to-hell look on your face. Oh, Christina, where's my love gone? If you really cared, you'd say I'll come with you anywhere, you'd come to me tonight and say to the devil with conventions – '

'Would I also say to the devil with your wife, Rob? Your poor sick wife who is dying? Would you really want me if I were that sort of woman?'

Again that twisted smile. 'Oh, I've had that sort of woman too, believe me,' he said with a weary sigh and released me. I walked towards the door.

'Where are you going?'

'Upstairs to my room.'

'I wasn't aware that I had dismissed you.'

'Then be aware now, Captain Robin Neal Cawdor Faro, that I am dismissing myself – '

There were footsteps outside and as Garnet entered the room, I wondered if he had overheard any of our conversation. I stared anxiously at him, but his face betrayed nothing other than a cold dislike for the man who stood there and whose presence he ignored.

Taking my hands he said: 'Welcome back, Christina. It's good to see you again.' And I felt sure he would have kissed me had his father not been watching.

'Well?' drawled Rob.

'Nothing is well. My mother wishes to see you. I came to see Christina.'

'There are things we must discuss first, Garnet.' From the

table, Rob lifted a sheaf of papers. 'Bills. As you will once again appreciate, the regular source of all communication between us.' There was an ugly set to his jaw and he swung round as if aware of my presence for the first time. 'That will be all, Miss Holly,' he said coldly. 'You may go now.'

That will be all. That is all. Everything is over, finished. I ran up to my room and only then did I give vent to my grief. Once I began to cry I could not stop but somewhere I must have slept with exhaustion, for it was almost dark when Mrs. Reed appeared with a tray.

'I thought perhaps ye'd like yours in your room, miss. I ken fine how terrible all this is for ye.'

I sat up and for a dreadful moment I thought she was referring to Rob's deception. 'Aye,' she continued, 'it's awfu' for us to see her like this, but sich a shock to ye, miss – the change in her when she was so well when you left her – '

I had no desire for food but gratefully drank the pot of tea. There was only one thing left for me now. I knew what I must do – leave Faro immediately, return to Monkshall. And then? But that was all my tortured mind could face. What happened next was beyond my reasoning, how I would put together the shattered ruins of my life.

I had hardly begun packing when the door opened and Rob stood there, a bottle of wine in his hand: 'And what do you think you're doing?'

'I'm packing.'

'So much is obvious. And where are you going?'

'Back to Monkshall.'

'Which you should never have left in the first place. In a little while, she,' he nodded down in the direction of Ruth's room, 'she will be past your solicitude, I'll be coming to you – and you could have saved yourself this most unfortunate encounter. May I ask what you intend to do once you reach Monkshall?'

'I don't know.'

'You're not, of course, forgetting that Monkshall belongs

132

to me, so I have a right to know how you intend behaving when you reach my house.'

'I don't know.'

He banged the bottle on the table and seized me roughly. 'You do know, by God, you do. I can see it clearly written in your face. You're going to leave me, aren't you? Going to make another life, forget all about Rob Neal, isn't that it? Wicked Rob Neal, who broke your heart by deceiving you.' He paused. 'Did I really deceive you? Think hard. Did I lie to you?'

'Yes.'

'When? You see you can't remember – because I never actually lied to you. Everything I said was truth, perhaps with omissions or evasions but still truth.'

'You told me that you were completely and absolutely mine, that I alone had your entire devotion, that I was the woman you loved to the exclusion of the whole world. No, no, Rob – not to the exclusion of the whole world. There's one woman has a prior claim, and as long as there's Ruth, as far as I'm concerned you belong to her – '

'As long as she's alive,' he said dryly. 'And that problem does not seem without solution. As for belonging to her, my dear girl, I have yet another shock for your sensibilities. I haven't belonged to her, as you so neatly put it, for twenty years, the time we have kept our separate establishments.'

He walked over to the window, stared across the garden, as if he saw some past pageant of his life enacted there. 'Love never existed on her side for me. She was betrothed to my elder brother Luke. She only took me, a besotted substitute, because he was drowned off the coast here and she needed a father for his unborn child. Once the ring was on her finger, she stopped pretending, she never forgave me for being the one who came back, she even built up a defence for her refusal to live with me, by pretending that I had let Luke die.'

Turning he leaned against the windowsill. 'Cruelty? Suffering? I've had it all and more. But it's all finished now – or so I thought.' Head on side he watched me. 'You say nothing.

How does this fit your little drama, eh? Was I supposed to sit around for twenty years with a woman who wanted to share the comforts of my home, social position, every little luxury she could have, without ever once recognising that I was also a man, a husband with other rights. Let me assure you, in case you have doubts, that it is utterly degrading for a husband to force his attentions upon an unwilling wife, and even the most passionate heart fails before what is virtually rape of one's legal spouse.'

He came to my side, seized my hands and held them against his breast. 'Ah, I see the warm flicker of compassion in your eyes – you have become human again. My dear, you are not the only one to know what it is like to be alone and unloved. Fortunately as a man I had access to other means of gratification through the years. Perhaps you would like to hear about them too, so that you can believe what a monster the man you love can be.' He laughed bitterly. 'I wish you could see the disgust on your face, there is no need for further words of mine – I can spare you my debaucheries and the dark side of Cawdor Faro.'

He went to the dressing-table and picked up my silver-backed hair brush, a long-ago birthday present from Sir Andrew. 'Perhaps one day you'll remember I have a better side too, a side which had compassion for a girl accused of murder, enough compassion to invite her to live here at Faro.' As he spoke he ran the soft bristles across his hand, the effect was disconcerting, oddly sensual.

'How forlorn your circumstance were, how pathetic, that first day in court. And how your brave stricken face began to haunt me, sleeping, waking. I longed to protect you and even when our eyes met so briefly, over so many heads, I felt – as if there was a strange communication.' He sighed. 'I've been sick, sick of these last years. If Ruth hadn't needed me, I think I would have left her long since, but she won even then. How do you walk out on a sick and dying woman who needs you and then,' he added brutally, 'is remarkably slow in the dying? I

134

have had to learn compassion too – that suddenly I could bear to be near her again, because I was sorry for her and instead of a wilful selfish woman, there was nothing left but a helpless sick child.'

He made a gesture towards me, but I sat down, staring at my empty ringless hands. Savagely he pulled me to my feet. 'By God, you won't ignore me like that. And I'll not let you go without a fight,' he said between clenched teeth.

His kisses devoured me with a passion to which my poor bruised senses began to respond because they were incapable of reasoning, of knowing right or wrong. They could only recognise as they had so often before, the warmth of his nearness, the strength and desire of his body, the illusion that told them this was love.

He released my mouth and almost gently pressed his face against my cheek. 'Don't go, my darling. I need you. I promise she won't last – I won't let her spoil this for us. I'll take on the responsibility of putting her out of her misery – '

'Don't – '

'Yes – I will – put her out of her misery and leave us free to marry if you promise to love me. I beg you to stay – dear heart, there's no need for you to go. Another day or two, and we'll be together for always. God, it wouldn't take much doing – I've shot an animal in less agony that hers – '

'Please, Rob, don't – don't sin your immortal soul. You couldn't be so cruel.'

'I could be monstrous cruel to anyone who came between us. At least stay until tomorrow, there might be great changes in our situation by then.'

Downstairs a clock chimed harmoniously. 'I must go, or Mrs. Reed will be wondering why I'm spending so much time in Miss Holly's bedroom. I'd better say you were upset and I was consoling you. How ironically true.' He went to the door. 'Oh, I almost forgot my wine.'

'Why did you bring it – don't tell me you were expecting a celebration?' I said angrily.

135

He weighed the bottle in his hand thoughtfully. 'No, this wine is for someone else. But we'll have our celebration – and soon. Never fear.' And the door closed behind him.

Sometime during that night while I dozed fitfully, I was awakened by Garnet shaking me gently. 'Wake up, Christina, wake up. It's mother – she's worse, I think she's dying. Please stay with her until I get the doctor. *He's* with her now,' he banged his fists together, 'I wish to God it was *he* who was lying there dying – how I would rejoice!' And his voice choked on a great sob of grief as he rushed blindly from the room.

I ran downstairs and opening the bedroom door saw them together for the first time. It was all I needed to jolt me into the full reality of my passion for this man, and its attendant folly. I was his slave, his creature, and where he was concerned, I was incapable of reasoning good from evil.

Even assuring myself that it was I whom he loved, to watch him holding Ruth close in his arms, Ruth the poor frail invalid, the unloved wife, heart almost leaped from body at the paroxysm of jealousy. Loathing myself for such a feeling, I knew that had he handed me the glass of wine and told me to give it to her, even knowing it was poisoned, at that moment I would have done as he commanded, without a single questioning glance. In fact, had I imagined then that he did indeed love his wife, that she might survive, I would have had her murder in my own heart. Alas, I saw all too clearly how other frail women before me – aye, and many still unborn, would become victims of their all-consuming love and the mastery of the evil men who possessed them.

He gave a curt nod in my direction. 'Get her to drink some of this,' he whispered, thrusting a glass of wine into my hands. 'It will help ease her.'

'No, no – I don't want it.'

'Come along now, it will do you good,' he said in the commanding manner of father to stubborn child.

'But it's so bitter – '

136

'Nonsense. It's the same wine as you usually drink, my dear. I brought it up specially for you.'

'I don't care –' Feebly she thrust the glass away. 'I don't want it, Christina,' she appealed to me, 'it has such a nasty taste.'

Our eyes met briefly over her head. 'Then Miss Holly will try some,' said Rob. I saw the quick desire blaze in his eyes and quickly change to mockery. His hand shook a little as he handed me the glass. 'An excellent Burgandy, Miss Holly, and usually my wife's favourite. See, my dear, Miss Holly doesn't think it's unpleasant, in fact, I think she rather likes it.'

I smiled stiffly but after a couple of sips laid it aside.

'You see,' said Ruth, 'She doesn't like it either. You see –'

'I see nothing, except that perhaps Miss Holly doesn't have your undeniable head for wines and spirits, my dear.'

'Alas, sir,' I said apologetically. 'You're quite right. I'm no judge and if you'll forgive me, I have very little taste for wine.'

I looked at him and saw reflected in his eyes the scene at dinner at the Cafe Royal, then the ride home to Monkshall with my head on his shoulder.

Ruth moved uncomfortably as though aware of the scene. 'I should like to be with Christina, now.'

Our hands touched briefly as with hardly a glance in my direction, he relinquished his pitiable burden. I touched the muscular forearm, saw a stubble of beard on his chin, the first light of dawn haloed his head for an instant and then he was gone from the room.

'Oh, it's good to have you back, my dear kind friend.'

'I'm glad to be here – and I promise I won't leave you again this time.'

'You promise? Oh –' and she began to cry softly. 'Oh, please give me your strength, give me your strength. Oh, Christina, what am I to do. Why does he hate me so?'

'Of course he doesn't hate you.'

'How do you know?' she said angrily, then added savagely, 'Of course he hates me. Everyone else in the house knows, so

I don't see why you shouldn't be told. Oh, I've tried to make amends but he won't listen. Why does he hate me – how can he hate me, even when I'm dying? We were happy once – for a little while. And when I first took ill, he was kind and considerate. I thought he had forgiven the wrong I did him, and it was almost worth being ill. But he can never forgive me that Garnet isn't his son – and worse that I haven't given him a son of his own.'

'Don't talk about it, dear, you're only upsetting yourself.'

'But I must tell someone – I must tell you.' She was silent for a moment. 'I wish I didn't love him so. At least even when I die, purgatory can't be any worse than what I've suffered on earth these past few years. Oh, he really turned the tables, once I realised I loved him as he had once loved me – in vain. Too late,' she sighed. 'And although I tried to make amends, I had hurt him once and now he was getting his full measure of revenge, every last ounce of it – '

'Ruth dear, you don't mean all this. You're feverish, that's all.'

'Feverish – I wish to God that *was* all. Oh, Christina, I love him, I love him. What in God's name am I going to do?'

And as I cradled her worn body, the frail bones of her in my arms, I too hated Rob at that moment. Suddenly she sat up. 'Well, I'm not going to die. I'm going to live. I'm no worse than I've been many times before and now that you're here I'm going to get better. I've decided,' she added with a sigh that would have been that of a spoilt and petulant child had the circumstances been less pathetic. 'In fact, Christina, I should like something nice – to eat and drink, to keep my strength up.'

'Tell me what you want and I'll get it for you.'

'Something sweet. There's some coffee cordial in the cupboard over there. He says I'm to take it like medicine and not drink it like wine but oh, it's so good. You must try some, it will cheer us both up. Get two glasses and I shall pour it, to show you how strong I am.'

138

To please her, I took a few sips, but it was too sweet and syrupy for my taste. She asked for a biscuit, refilled her glass twice and drank the contents. At last she seemed more restful.

'I'm tired now,' she said with a yawn, 'I think I'll close my eyes for a while.'

'Would you like me to stay with you?'

'Oh, would you – please? It's such a comfort to have you near me.'

'Very well then, I'll get a blanket and lie down on the chaise-longue here.'

I took the wine glasses, washed and dried them and replaced the cordial in the cupboard. For a moment I looked at that wine bottle and telling myself that what I did was innocent I took it along to the water closet and poured the contents away. When I returned to the bedroom, she was sleeping peacefully and making myself as comfortable as possible, I never thought to sleep, although my legs were heavy and I found myself staggering as I carried blanket and pillow to my couch.

I had not the slightest recollection of closing my eyes, and it wasn't until long afterwards that I wondered how a light sleeper like myself never moved during the doctor's visit, nor did I awaken when Mrs. Reed came in and after one swift glance at Ruth, shook me awake and sent for the Captain.

I knew I must awaken but seemed drugged with sleep. I had a dream of Rob holding Ruth in his arms, I heard their voices but it was as if I fought my way towards them through immense clouds of heavy mist.

'Wake up, wake up do,' cried Mrs. Reed, and finally roused me into a sitting position. 'The mistress – the mistress – '

I looked over at the bed and saw Rob clasping Ruth in his arms.

'Say it, Cawdor darling. Say it, please – tell me just once that you love me. Tell me before I go – have pity, Cawdor – my love.'

He gave a great sigh and raising his head looked in my direction, his face twisted, ugly, like a wild thing at bay. Then he laid his lips against her cheek. I saw the words shaped, heard her sigh, then his mouth covered hers. In that second, unable to tear my eyes away, time itself seemed frozen. They were both still, two fair heads on a single pillow, and I knew that she was dead.

Mrs. Reed, sobbing noisily, took her gently from his arms. 'I'll make her comfortable, sir, just as I've always done.'

He hovered by her side. 'What can I do?'

Through a great veil I saw Mrs. Reed watching me. 'See to Miss Holly, Captain. Take her back to her room, the poor lassie looks like enough to die herself.' And she began to cry again, rocking poor Ruth in her arms.

With his arm under my elbow supporting me, Rob led the way upstairs and closed the bedroom door behind us. Turning he took me in his arms, held me hard against him. His hands caressed, implored – 'I want you – I want you so.' His voice was rough with desire.

'No, no – Rob, not here – '

'What difference does it make – I'm a free man now?'

'Rob – oh my darling – how could you?'

'How could I? I want to love you now – this moment, but you never forget, do you? To you it would be the unforgivable sin to come to your lover – your future husband while his wife's body was still warm.' He released me. 'Get some sleep,' he said coldly, 'you're going to need it.'

'Rob – ' I said.

But without turning, he shook his head and left me.

I fell upon my bed, wept, and again somewhere I must have slept, for I awoke with Mrs. Reed bringing in a breakfast tray and the clock downstairs striking eleven. She bore signs of copious weeping, and when I apologised for oversleeping, and asked what I could do, she said:

'Nothing, nothing at all, miss. You made her last hours

happy and now she's at rest with our Good Lord. Aye, she even had her death wish that the Captain would love her again and that she would go to eternity in his arms.' She shook her head sadly. 'There's been some awfu' talk these past years about how things were betwixt them. Aye, I'm glad they were reconciled at the end.'

'Poor Captain Faro,' I said, gathering some conventional condolence was required of me.

Mrs. Reed shook her head. 'I wouldna' waste too much sympathy on the Captain, ye ken. He'll no suffer for long. We'll soon enough be hearing he's married again.'

I was wondering with a little amusement if Mrs. Reed had the second sight or if the main participants in the drama had given the game away.

'Aye,' she continued, 'there's been rumours,' she paused, looked at me, thought for a moment before adding, 'Ach well, it's none o' my business, but there's no need for ye to waste yer sympathy on the Captain,' she repeated and firmly closed her mouth, in the manner of one who has said too much already.

'What rumours?' I asked.

'Well, there's a woman – Edinburgh way, a woman he's been keeping for years – and I hear tell he's been just waiting for the mistress's death to marry her. Not before time, either, ye'll gather.' She lowered her voice to a whisper. 'I understand there's a second family – a wee girl and another bairn who must be born by now – Miss, miss – '

I heard her voice from far off, and when I opened my eyes again she was pushing smelling salts under my nose.

'Ach, miss, ye fainted clean away then. I'm no' surprised at all.' I looked up at her in horror. What had I done, had I given myself away? Then I remembered what had made me faint. Not Rob's love, nor Ruth's death, but the housekeeper's revelation that the Captain was all set to marry his mistress near Edinburgh who had already borne him a child – with another on the way.

141

'Aye, you've had a shocking time, shocking. You tak' it easy – when ye're feeling a wee thing better, the Captain wishes to speak with you in the morning-room.'

Assuring her I was better already and that all would be well when I ate something, as soon as the door closed, I thrust the tray aside. For a moment I stared at my stricken face in the mirror, but there was nothing but a miracle could restore laughter or warmth again to the horror-filled eyes before me. As I went downstairs dragging my legs like an old woman, I found myself realising that perhaps I had always known. Two facets of his mysterious behaviour stood out clearly pointing to the truth. First, that my benefactor Captain Cawdor Faro knew all about Monkshall. Second, when as Rob Neal, he arrived late one night, muddy and dishevelled, there was evidence of some female entanglement in the face powder on his coat, the musky perfume clinging to his hair – and the three neat scratches down his cheek, which could readily be attributed to fingernails.

I found him leaning against the mantelpiece regarding the ashes of last night's fire. His face was in shadow. 'I want you to leave the house immediately,' he said brusquely, 'but there are some things we must discuss first.'

I held my hands together tightly, to stop them trembling. So this was it. In a few moments he would be telling me it was all over between us. 'At last, Rob. At last, the truth.'

His head turned towards me fiercely. 'What the devil are you talking about now?'

'I understand that I'm to commiserate with you – offer you condolences on one hand and congratulations on the other.'

'Congratulations – what the devil are you talking about?'

'Rumour has it that, like Elsinore, the House of Faro is to have the "funeral baked-meats to coldly furnish forth the marriage-table".'

'Wh – at?' Hands on hips he stared at me, his face incredulous. 'They can't possibly know about that?'

'Everyone does – everyone but me, it appears, knows that

142

you are contemplating an early marriage to a lady who lives near Edinburgh – whom it would appear has two excellent reasons at least, for expecting such a marriage.'

He came over and took my hands. 'My darling girl, what on earth are you raving about? Of course, we're to be married but – reasons? I don't understand – '

'Neither do I, Rob, neither do I understand the reasons why you haven't warned me that you already have a mistress – who would appear to have a prior claim on you – '

He threw back his head and laughed. 'Madeline! Oh, for God's sake, so they know about Madeline!'

Where was my miracle now? The miracle that there was some plausible explanation, that rumour had lied. 'And which life does she fit into – what name does she call her lover? Are you Rob Neal or Captain Cawdor Faro to her?'

He shook his head solemnly, all laughter gone. 'Servants, damned servants,' he whispered. 'I'd forgotten, my dear, that you would be accessible from your position in my household to the gossip of the servants' hall. And also young Garnet, doubtless, would do anything he could to twist a knife in my back. Sit down.' When I protested, he thrust me roughly into a chair. 'Sit down, when I tell you to – and since you're so eager to hear the full story, by God, you shall. Her name is Madeline Meade – ah, I see you know her – '

'Only by reputation. Her sister is a near neighbour of Monkshall.'

'Oh yes, the gallant Miss Meade, patroness of the arts, famous for her soirées.'

I looked at him. 'And, of course, the reason why you knew so much about Sir Andrew and life at Monkshall.'

He shrugged. 'In the beginning of our association it was a necessary refuge to spare Ruth's feelings, but eventually the lady was indiscreet, some letters forwarded to Faro, and thanks to my fool of a clerk, the cat was well and truly out of the bag.'

And now I understood why the unfortunate man, terrified

of provoking another outburst of his master's wrath, had been scared out of his wits to forward Ruth's letters addressed to me at Monkshall, without precise instructions first from his employer. His confrontation with stern Mr. Mackintosh must have been equally upsetting.

Rob had lit a cigar and for a few moments contemplated its spiral of smoke before continuing, as if the matter was of no more importance than a casual after-dinner conversation between us:

'Yes, Madeline has been my mistress for ten years now. Ten whole years,' he added sardonically, 'cancelled out – like that,' he said with a snap of his fingers, 'as if they had never existed, the first day I saw you in Edinburgh. Dare after that to say I don't love you. If we hadn't met – or let us say had I not been determined to have you and contrived a meeting between us – I should have married Madeline, although my feelings for her have undergone some considerable change in the last few years. I have discovered that she is constitutionally incapable of remaining faithful to me when I am away, and I have been left with less than the passion – or hope – with which one enters marriage.'

'There is a – family, I believe,' I said stiffly. 'Don't you owe them something?'

He shook his head sadly. 'Had our daughter lived, I would have seen marriage to her mother as my duty. But alas, I seem to be as unlucky in fatherhood as I am in love. Isobel died of scarlet fever on the day after her fifth birthday. I have never quite recovered from an exquisitely beautiful little girl breathing her last in my arms.' He bit his lips, turning his face from me. 'Things began to go badly between Madeline and myself after that. There were constant quarrels and equally constant reconciliations. From one of these our second child was conceived and the week after I first saw you in that gloomy Edinburgh court Madeline gave birth to my son. My son, Christina, my only son, who lived for five days.'

He covered his eyes with his hands and it was then that I

144

went to him and took him in my arms, cradling him like a child against my heart. It was the only time I ever remember being strong in our relationship, and I can still see it clearly, every detail, the bones of his skull pressed against my breast and far below us the booming of the sea like the sound of our own heartbeats.

The storm passed and he said calmly: 'Like all men I am something of an emotional coward. I had to be sure she would not suffer too cruelly by my rejection before I could dismiss her. I have been delighted to discover that since spring she has been as bored with me as I am with her, and that I am no longer the only man in her life. However, like all women, she felt I should be punished for the withdrawal of my affections, and she would have liked to have had both myself and her new lover as willing slaves, playing one against the other. When she discovered that was not to be the case, hurt pride and the loss of a sizable income from me made her react with considerable violence.' He paused. 'On the night I arrived at Monkshall so unexpectedly, I wanted to tell you the truth – I tried to will you to let me stay, but my virtuous little Christina – how would you have taken such a confession? So I lied instead, about the accident. She threw me out of her carriage, which I had given her as a present, incidentally – '

There was a ring at the front door. Rob stood up, buttoned his coat, ran a hand across his hair. 'I must go – and so must you.'

'Yes, there will be a lot to do.'

'You misunderstand me completely, my dear. It is my wish that you leave this house immediately.'

'But the funeral – '

'Need not concern you. It is for the family only.'

'But I was her friend. She would have wanted – '

'My dear Christina, what my late wife would have wanted or not wanted is immaterial. You are now my only concern – '
He held me for a brief moment and said: 'Oh my love, please go. Go now.'

'Won't it seem strange?'

He smiled. 'I assure you it will seem a lot stranger if you stay under my roof for another night. My darling, you don't understand, do you? I'm not a good actor, and how do you expect me to get through almost a week of pretence that we are not in love with each other? Let me assure, you, there are some very sharp eyes at Faro. So, for my sake, Christina, go back to Monkshall and wait for me there.'

'But what shall I say to Mrs. Reed – to Garnet?'

'Garnet won't be back until late this evening. As for Mrs. Reed – and for them both, you can blame it on the Captain – or let me do so. I'll indulge in some small drama, hint that we had a difference of opinion. That you spoke your mind too firmly over my treatment of Ruth. They'll love that – and certainly believe anything bad of me. Anyway, they'll never question – they're all terrified of the Captain.'

He walked over to the bellpull with his arm around my shoulders. As we waited he kissed me gently, ran a finger tenderly down my cheek. 'And that, my darling, must last you until our next meeting.' Taking out his watch he consulted it. 'Expect me two weeks from today at three o'clock in the afternoon. I'll be at Monkshall with a minister to marry us – ' He held my hand tightly and released it as Mrs. Reed knocked on the door.

'Miss Holly is to leave immediately,' he said sternly. 'Please summon Broom and have him drive her to Aberdeen station.'

'Yes, Captain,' said Mrs. Reed with an anxious glance in my direction.

He picked up his half-finished cigar, blew smoke. 'That will be all, Miss Holly, you may go now. Good-day to you.'

Speechless I followed Mrs. Reed into the corridor, up the stairs. 'Miss, I thought you'd be staying,' she said in a shocked voice. 'She would have wanted you to.' A pause. 'Have you had words, miss?' When I nodded she said: 'Oh, I can see he's upset you – he's an awfu' man. And after you being so good to the mistress – '

146

'Mrs. Reed.'

We turned to find him staring up at us from the hall. 'Yes, Captain.'

'Be so good as to stop gossiping to Miss Holly – I'm sure she'll appreciate that there's much to be done and the sooner we are rid of her the more efficiently we'll proceed.'

He bowed and turning on his heel, disappeared down the corridor.

'Tch, tch, Miss Holly,' muttered Mrs. Reed angrily.

'Please don't worry,' I said.

'Aye, it'll be because he's so upset, right enough – '

'Will you please explain to Garnet that I had to leave without saying goodbye? – '

I remember little of the journey back to Monkshall, except that it was a calm beautiful day and when we crossed the River Tay at Dundee, there were seals basking on the sandbanks, and a line of porpoises followed our progress, leaping in and out of the shadow the train and high bridge cast on the smooth waters far below.

9

At Monkshall, preparing for a wedding I was certain would never take place, my moods varied from tortured disbelief to brief elation, in which I accepted the event as one would a miracle. Alas, I failed to recognise that we each carry within us our own miracles alike with the seeds of our own destruction, inseparable from the moment of birth.

My self-torments were happily in vain for punctually at three o'clock two weeks after Ruth's death a carriage appeared on the drive. From it emerged Rob accompanied by Mr. Mackintosh and a minister of the Church of Scotland. Ten minutes later with hardly a greeting between us, the wedding ceremony was performed, and so the fantasy dream which began for me in an Edinburgh courtroom on a cold spring day became reality on a warm July afternoon in the flower-decked drawing-room at Monkshall.

In the little time that lay ahead before storm clouds of suspicion and fear gathered on the horizon, I often awoke in the early morning, first at Monkshall, then in the ship that carried us to Greece, and somewhat belatedly I began to appreciate the gipsy lore my ancestors had bequeathed me. How otherwise to account for the sleeping man at my side, the fair head on the pillow beside me? Only later was I to recognise that magic has two faces, white and black, that it can be worked for evil too as well as good.

That honeymoon voyage down the Mediterranean belongs to a chronicle of its own, for it has but a brief part to play in this story, and the inane but brief dalliance of two people in love has little to amuse or interest any but the two principals.

Suffice to indulge the curious that the joys Rob promised at our betrothal in the gardens of Monkshall, I found. And I had little reason to regret that I was not the first woman in his life. Experience had taught him to be a skilful and accomplished lover, making the brief physical fulfilment of the passion between us extend into prolonged ecstasy to those boundless frontiers where soul and body belong together no more. The joy and delight we found in each other's bodies extended to the satisfaction of more intellectual realms. In books and music, love of the countryside, a shared sense of laughter – in particular, a sometimes earthy humour at ourselves and the human predicament. It was a pleasant revelation that promised when some day we quit these golden shores of love for younger lovers, the memory of the bright blue sky and azure sea of those first days of marriage would be but a curtain raised upon a mature relationship, with understanding and companionship to enhance the tenderness of love.

Exotic shores, horizoned with palm trees and white houses shimmering in heat haze gave place to less romantic and agreeable prospects of noisy, strange – and not always sweet – smelling harbours packed with boats and flies and dirt, with squalour and heathen tongues substituting for distant and more preferable enchantments. At last we sailed into Piraeus which exuded little of the glories of Ancient Greece but a good deal of the commerce, squalour and vice of the modern world.

'Wait until you see Athens,' said Rob, as I settled thankfully into the carriage, leaving the port with its beggars and the screaming children who had besieged us, far behind. 'Wait until you see Athens, that will change your mind.'

Our hotel was overlooked by the Acropolis, magical and eternal upon the heights above the town. We explored it by moonlight, leaping like children, full of laughter and mischief, darting in and out of the pillars of the ancient temples. Then we took a carriage and drove out to Delphi, past Mount Olympus, whose thick woods seemed older than time itself.

150

There were no birds to haunt twisted boughs and a dark forbidding silence hushed each echo of sky.

'Don't you feel that anything might happen, that the gods and goddesses might suddenly appear over that hill, with Pan playing his pipes and centaurs trotting out of the dark undergrowth there?'

Wine-bottle in hand, Rob chuckled. 'Why are your whispering, do you think they might hear you?'

I shivered. 'Yes, I feel them everywhere – eyes watching, ears listening.'

Rob laughed. 'Well, at least let us give them a scene of which they will approve – wine and love – ' He took me in his arms, but I couldn't concentrate on kissing him, with this – awareness – of that other world. 'Ah, what you need is some wine and some good solid food,' he said, unpacking the picnic hamper.

Two days afterwards I took ill with fever, a sweating aching fever with acute stomach pains. Rob sent for a British doctor, and as I writhed in agony he pronounced the cause as food poisoning.

'Very common in these parts in summer, it's the flies, I'm afraid.' He was very matter-of-fact about being called out so urgently and thrust a box of pills into Rob's hand. 'These should do the trick.'

The hotel was no longer luxurious or inviting. It was hot and miserable and the bed conjured up strange nightmares, the hallucinations that fever in a strange country bring. Once I dreamed that Ruth was alive again, and I watched Rob pouring red wine into a glass and forcing it between her lips. As it ran down her chin like blood, I knew it was poisoned and I awoke screaming.

Rob was sitting by my bedside, reading and smoking a cigar in the dim light. He bathed my head with a cold towel, and as I protested at such menial rites he laughed: 'Not at all, my dear, I insist on being your nursemaid, too, besides you're far too precious a burden to relinquish into any other hands.

151

They may run to British doctors in Athens, but I imagine that British nurses are something of a rarity.'

One night when the fever was at its height, I thought I dreamed of Rob flicking small white pellets into a wineglass, and when I screamed:

'You're poisoning me!'

He laughed. 'It isn't as bad as that, my dear. These are what the doctor left to make you feel better.'

And this time I knew I was wide awake. Reluctantly taking the glass from him and draining its bitter contents, I knew also that whatever he and the doctor maintained, I was getting no better, only worse each day, as added to sickness came deplorable weakness and lassitude.

'How are you this morning?' he would ask hopefully.

'Worse. I'll never be better. I'm sure I'm going to die here.'

'Nonsense – you're not going to die anywhere. It's just a passing malaise.'

'But I want to go home. When can we go home?'

He sighed. 'As soon as a ship arrives.'

Too ill to read, too weak to dress, Rob's absences increased as he searched for a ship to take us back to Britain, and I lay on a couch all day long, sometimes staggering to the balcony, listening to the babble of voices below. Among the strange faces I tried to fasten imagination on one individual, whose hopes and joys, fears and pleasures, might not be so different from my own, where only the colourful world was remote and the customs alien.

Friendless and sorry for myself, I also managed to spare a thought for my husband, now quiet, withdrawn, all laughter had died between us and when we were together, apart from nursing me, he took refuge in reading on the balcony, smoking incessantly. Knowing he was unhappy, I would make a special effort to take a bath, make myself look attractive for him, but such effort was enough to send me fevered back again to bed. On other days such labours seemed hardly worth the reward of the thin hollow-eyed wraith who stared so fretfully from my mirror. Gone was the healthy gipsy look, all that remained were huge haunted eyes, dark-ringed in a white face, and a wild profusion of black hair streaming over my shoulders, for I could not bear its weight fastened high upon my head, in the current fashion.

And sometimes imagination painted a ghost lurking behind my ravaged reflection, the mocking ghost of Ruth Faro, who had in her turn loved Cawdor Faro not wisely but too late and too well.

Worn out, exasperated by my pleadings and his vain daily search at the port, Rob had decided that we must make the journey back by land, when we had news of a ship. How eagerly I directed him to pack our luggage, how delightedly from the carriage I watched the last of the hotel, shorn alas of the remotest possibility of any sentimental honeymoon memories.

Weak and tearful with relief at the prospect of seeing Scotland again, perhaps heartened that I was not after all, like poor Lord Byron, doomed to die in Greece, I even recovered a little once we were at sea. After some days of unbroken sunshine, misted horizons and only the faintest nausea, I wondered if all my terrors had been in vain.

However, even without the daily sickness that had plagued me, I concluded that my illness must have been of a serious nature, for I was still too weak and languid to do more than sit quietly in the shade on deck.

Rob could not have done more, he fetched and carried shawls, rugs and books. He read to me often, but sometimes through half-closed eyes, pretending to be asleep, I would study him, catch him watching me anxiously, but at the same time biting his lips with a sullen frown. Or I would fancy he watched over me as a doctor watches a patient to whom he cannot tell the truth. Sometimes alone I wept, for the situation was well removed from our bridal voyage on these waters, and this woman bore no relationship to the happy high-spirited bride who had accompanied Rob then. At other times, I remembered that twenty years ago he had taken Ruth to Piraeus, and I wondered whether all her illness, like mine, had begun through some unfortunate contact on that ill-fated shore.

I was never so happy in my life as on the day the coast of Scotland was sighted and we watched it together. 'Tomorrow night we'll sleep at Monkshall,' said Rob, 'and all our troubles will be over.'

Perhaps through excitement I was sick again, and by the time we reached home I was so weak that Rob carried me bodily from the carriage upstairs to the great bed, while Mrs. Maxwell fluttered anxiously in the background, exclaiming how poorly I looked and quite shocked, wringing her hands over my exhaustion.

'No, you can't get her anything,' said Rob sharply. 'All she needs to do is sleep.' He kissed my forehead. 'I'll get Dr. James here tomorrow.'

When I re-opened my eyes, a day and a night had passed and there was the doctor standing by my bed. When he asked, as doctors do, what was the trouble, I moaned.

'I think I'm going to die.'

During the examination that followed, he asked many questions, especially about the duration and symptoms of my illness. 'It does indeed sound like food poisoning – perhaps some contaminated sea-food, to which you were unaccustomed.'

'Well, am I going to die?'

He laughed. 'No, dear lady, indeed you are not. I am happy to say you have quite recovered from any trace of food poisoning. We must turn our thoughts to another source for your present malaise.' And with eyes twinkling he took my hands 'This malaise, I fear, is one that has bedevilled females since time began and will go on until time ends. It's an illness from which they make a remarkable – and, may I say, a blooming recovery?'

'You mean – ?'

'I suspect that you're going to have a baby, and food poisoning unfortunately combined with the sickness of early pregnancy is to blame for your present unfortunate condition. However, a few more weeks – let me see, once you are safely into your third month, you should begin to feel a great deal better,' he added cheerfully.

'And what did the doctor say?' asked Rob, when he arrived back from St. Bernard's Crescent where the problems of the export business had accumulated in his absence. 'I must say you're looking much better. What pretty hair.'

'It's not quite dry. Mrs. Maxwell helped me wash it. And oh – how wonderful to have my own bathtub again.'

'This is quite miraculous. I go away and leave you sick to death and return home to find your eyes dancing and quite your old self again, looking as if the whole business was just a bad dream.'

'Sit down, darling,' I said. 'Come along, sit down.' I took his hand. 'I have some news for you. The doctor is almost sure that I'm going to have a baby.'

'You mean, all that sickness was just pregnancy. I don't believe it.'

'There were other symptoms too, Rob,' I reminded him gently, 'but I thought it was because of being so sick that I was late, not the other way round. Darling, are you pleased? You're looking so glum. Why don't you say something.'

'I haven't had a chance, have I?' He smiled with effort. 'Of course, I'm delighted, but I'm also quite speechless. I can't think of anything suitable to say for such an occasion. I'll have to get used to the idea first.'

It was disappointing, hardly the reception I had expected, and I felt as if I had been cheated of what I imagined would be the devoted husband's reaction to impending parenthood. After all, I could hardly excuse his ill-concealed dismay on the grounds that he was a young man who knew little of the facts of life, or had never begotten a child before. Of course, Garnet was not his son, but then I thought of Madeline and

155

her two children by him. And I wondered jealously how he had received similar news from her. Indeed, his distress seemed more appropriate to such news from mistress than from his wife. I discovered that a tear was trickling down my cheek.

'Darling, what's wrong now?'

'Nothing,' I sniffed. 'I thought you'd be so pleased.'

'And so I am. Only I had hoped we would have a little more time together before your illness merged into pregnancy and a baby came along. I am selfish enough to enjoy having you all to myself at the very beginning of our marriage.'

'If you feel that way about it, then you might have done something to prevent me having a baby. After all, you're a man of experience,' I said angrily. 'You must know only too well how such matters are managed. And I can assure you I would have been happy to wait for a year or two – and to miss all that miserable sickness when I should have been enjoying my honeymoon.'

'I hardly think it's fair to blame me, when you obviously enjoyed our love-making just as much as I did – '

'Oh, what a thing to say – '

'For heaven's sake, Christina, spare me the false modesty of a fashionable pretence that you merely endure the marital bed in patient martyrdom to wifely duty – '

'I didn't say that – '

'Well, don't – ever. The prudery of outraged matrons ill becomes my wild gipsy girl.' Suddenly his teasing manner vanished and a frown of impatience I had learned to recognise and respect took its place. 'I will not endure it, you know. You needn't expect me to make love to you in the dark, swathed in blankets up to your neck. I warn you – I will certainly leave you – '

'Oh – Rob – no – '

The next moment I was close in his arms, we were both saying we were sorry, laughing, crying together over our first quarrel.

156

'Whoever heard of two married people going on in such a manner about an event that was only to be expected,' said Rob. 'I do love you, Christina, and I am pleased. It's wonderful to think that I may soon have a son of my own.'

For a little while my health improved, apart from the deplorable weakness which made me totally incapable of running Monkshall. I was glad indeed that Rob had turned over the housekeeping to Mrs. Maxwell, who had in her turn invested in some sturdy help from the village. I discovered that the slightest exertion left me exhausted, and if I were to get through the evening when Rob returned from Edinburgh and fulfil the wifely duty of being 'blithe at bed and board' which he expected since my return to health, it meant doing little in Monkshall. I dare not tell him that such energetic pursuits which we both found so pleasant took their toll. I wanted him to believe that I was completely well again. It was a happy lie, a pretence to keep his content too.

At last when I thought all danger was passed, I awoke one morning in considerable pain, and the sight of blood had Mrs. Maxwell rushing for the doctor from the village. He looked grave and asked that a consultant should be called in. After an examination, they adjourned with Rob, and when they returned I realised with horror that my life might be in danger, that there was some possibility that my unborn child might murder me as I had murdered my own mother.

'There is nothing else for it, sir, if your wife is to keep this baby and her own health, for the next few months at least and perhaps even until spring, she must live the life of an invalid. She must have absolute peace and rest,' he ended sternly.

'You must do as the doctor orders, my dear,' said Rob, moving his bed into the nearest guest-room. When I protested, he said: 'Absolute peace and rest, remember – '

'Please stay with me. I don't want you to go.'

'I am only across the corridor if you need me. My darling, don't you understand at all? I must go. I love you – normally pregnancy wouldn't make any difference to our love-making, but this is different, your life – and the baby's might be in danger. It's not a bit of use crying, we must face facts – and one undeniable fact is that I can't be near you all night and never touch you. Allow me that much humanity.'

His absence at night made me very depressed and sorry for myself. I too felt somehow cheated of the happy intimacy of those early weeks of marriage. I had envisaged the thrill of pregnancy, and once it was confirmed had expected a euphoric state, not just dragging weariness, more sickness and pain.

September passed and, the harvest carried home, over the whole landscape the sun sank low but the days were still mellow and warm. Mornings came when trees in the frost-bound woods burst into a shining spectrum of every shade from palest lemon to deepest crimson. Then one day from the North Sea the storms swept inland and the trees were stripped bare to their shining silver trunks, leaves swirled past the windows of the drawing-room, covering the green lawns with their multi-coloured quilt, while blackbirds darted across shrilly claiming territorial rights. And the last roses shed their petals like drops of blood in a grey and desolate world.

The evenings drew in and the fires inside Monkshall grew larger. As I sat sewing I noticed Rob often watched me, with a puzzled look, and I wondered as he swiftly averted his eyes from my glance whether he was comparing the irony of fate, which had exchanged him one invalid wife for another. I thought often of Ruth, especially when I was alone in the house, and remembered how once she too had been happy and reckless, then after Garnet's birth, beset by illness and the ravages of disease. I tried to forget the other part of the story, that Rob had once loved her, envying his brother and anxious enough to marry her himself. Had she responded to his love in time, he would doubtless have forgiven her for Garnet, for he was not a vindictive man and indeed seemed always to be one who had infinite toleration for the frailties of man – and woman – kind.

It was when I recalled Ruth that I grew cold with a chilly premonition that I too might be an invalid for life. How then his love would die so that one day he would take active measures to be free, beginning perhaps gently with lies to save my feelings and eventually growing careless with another mistress like Madeline, for I had already discovered that he was still, at forty-two, very attractive to women. I had also discovered that he was the kind of man who improves with age.

It would be better to be dead than have him cease to love me. And with that dire threat in mind, I stirred myself to do something to improve the condition of our life together. On a late October afternoon, Rob announced that his ship the 'King Robert' was in Granton that weekend and so I came to a melancholy decision. I must send him away, away from his restless pacing, his reading. When he did not have a book, a newspaper or cigar in his hand, he stood eternally by the window like a man who waits for some sign, and all the time I felt he scanned that horizon for a glimpse of the sea.

Only when storms swept the garden did he seem truly happy and as I watched huddled by the window above, he would rejoice in the wind's hustle, walking back and fro, back and fro, his face lifted to the elements. Occasionally he would swing round, leaning against the wind, eyes narrowed, his body swaying as if he stood in imagination on the bridge of his ship. He was a captive upon land, a prisoner, this man who had bragged once of never spending more than a few weeks at a time on land since his boyhood.

I knew yet another pang of jealousy for this rival no woman could defeat, this first mistress had never lost her eternal fascination for him – the sea. As his daily absences from Monkshall lengthened, I knew sadly that I would look for the last time on my carefree bridegroom and if I were not careful, for the last time on my contented husband. Only by returning him to the sea that he loved, could I keep him for ever.

When he announced that the ship would be leaving for Amsterdam as soon as they found a skipper, I asked: 'And when does she return?'

'In time for Christmas.'

I put in a few more stitches on the baby-gown I was sewing. 'Rob, will you do something for me?'

'Of course, when have I refused?' he said with the sweet ironic smile which so transformed his whole countenance, removing it from severity to loving kindness.

'Rob, I want you to take the ship to Amsterdam.'

He shook his head. 'Now, you know that isn't possible, my dear.'

'Yes, it is. I'm feeling much better and I have Mrs. Maxwell to take care of me.'

He looked at me thoughtfully, even joyfully, as if considering it, then his face darkened and he shook his head firmly. 'No.'

'Please, darling, it would do you so much good.'

'I'm not the one who is needing good done. You're the ill one.'

'And neither of us can forget it. Say then, that it will do our marriage more good if you go back to sea, than if you stay here where every day I see you beset by further irritations. Domesticity was never meant to be your role in life, Captain Cawdor Faro.'

'You really want me to go? You really think you could manage without me?'

'Yes.'

'Am I such a trial to you? I'm sorry but I think I warned you right at the beginning that I never have been a good actor. If I could be spared,' he considered for a moment. 'There are things I should do in Amsterdam that I can't rely on – '

I thought the matter was settled then, but in the week that

followed, first he was going, then he was not, until the main subject of our disagreements was my insistence and his numerous changes of mind. On another matter, he was quite determined.

'Once the baby is born, I've decided we shall return to Faro. I miss the place sorely. It is my home after all and I have a feeling for that wild Buchan coast, the home of my ancestors, that I can never arouse for Monkshall. Even being in the morning-room at Faro is like being on the sea. I had thought to give it to Garnet, as compensation for not really being his father, but now that we are to have a family, perhaps he would settle for Monkshall instead. Remind me to discuss it with Mr. Mackintosh when he comes on Thursday.'

After Ruth's death, Mrs. Reed retired and returned to Nairn. Garnet had gone to America to seek his fortune in the west and the great house awaited, dark, shuttered, with only the sea for ever echoing through its empty rooms. I would miss Monkshall which I infinitely preferred, however it was really of little consequence which house we occupied as long as Rob and I were together and happy.

Since our return, Mr. Mackintosh had been a constant visitor. On nights when I retired early I left the lonely old bachelor playing chess with Rob. His life compiled of startling revelations, I gathered he had accepted without the slightest indication of surprise, my husband's confession on the eve of our wedding that Rob Neal concealed the identity of Christina Holly's mysterious benefactor, Captain Cawdor Faro.

There was so much to do before Rob left for Amsterdam that he would sometimes be exasperated with us all and show the irritation which had given him such a reputation as an 'awfu' man to work for', among the servants at Faro. And it was with something of relief all round that they watched him ride off to join his ship. For me, the world and Monkshall seemed empty and as if the very weather mourned his absence, several days of incessant rain and leaden skies imprisoned

161

me within the house, deprived of my daily walk across the leaf-shrouded lawns to the sheltered warmth of the walled garden.

Then the sun returned and one morning while I was in the stables a shadow fell across my path, the shadow of an old gipsy woman with a basket over her arm. Her face was walnut-like in colour and texture, her teeth worn down to stumps blackened with chewing tobacco, her body stooped and ancient like a tree that has survived many storms. But there was shrewd wisdom in the still bright black eyes, a touch of gaiety in gold earrings and a red bandana tied over her white hair.

I knew Mrs. Maxwell would send her away, for she was 'always afraid of encouraging gipsies and being besieged by beggars', but my heart warmed toward one of my own blood.

'So you're the mistress of the house,' she said although there was nothing in my appearance of grey dress and black shawl to warrant such distinction. When I smiled assent, waiting for an offer of clothes pegs or some trinket from the basket, or a palm-reading, she put down the basket with a weary sigh, flexing hands twisted with rheumatism and age.

'Have you come far?'

'From Dunbar, my lady.'

'Dunbar – but that's miles away. Did you walk all the way?'

'Aye, and two days it's taken me. I'm not as fleet of foot as I was once.'

'You must be tired, come inside the house and I'll make you a cup of tea.'

'Tea,' she smiled broadly. 'Aye, I could do with that, my lady. Tea – and maybe a bite o' bread for naught has passed my lips since yestermorn.'

'You shall have more than bread. There's soup and meat,' I said, leading her into the kitchen where I sat her down at the table like a queen, while I waited on her, oblivious of

162

the scandalised expressions of the servants and Mrs. Maxwell's reproachful frown.

She ate hungrily, with intense concentration, eyes closed savouring each morsel and swallowing it with a contented sigh, so that I wondered if 'yestermorn' was her normal predicament. Swiftly I raided the larder for left-over pie, scones and cake, which I made into a parcel and put on top of her basket.

'Bless your dear kind heart, my lady. Now I must give you something in return.' And she took the basket and tipped out half the pegs on to the table.

'Please, no, I must pay you for them. Perhaps you would like to tell my fortune.'

She studied me for a moment, and shook her head. 'They're yours, my lady, and as for your fortune – well, I don't tell fortunes, I haven't the gift – I only tell things to Gorgio ladies who will believe anything as long as I make it sound nice and give them their money's worth. But to one of my own kind,' she shrugged, 'if I told you what fate has in store you wouldn't believe it, if I told you only the good things – and if I told you bad ones, you might pretend not to believe, but you would worry just the same.'

I smiled. 'That is the exact reason why I have never wanted to know.'

She nodded eagerly. 'So I was right. I'll tell you this much. Your man will come home safe from the sea, a Gorgio man with fair hair. You might have been happier with one of your own kind,' she added with a sigh, 'for you weren't born to the life you have here.' She glanced at my thickened waistline. 'The baby you carry is a son. For the rest, your fate was written on the day you were born and there is naught any but God in his mercy can do to change it now.'

From her pocket she brought out two gold coins. 'Ear-rings – for you,' she said pressing them into my hand. 'I have carried these for many a long day, my lady. Aye, take them, they are yours – they belonged to your mother. I knew you

163

were her bairn the moment I saw you. She died giving you birth right over there,' she said pointing in the direction of the stable.

'Oh, did you know her? Tell me about her – '

She shook her head. 'I cannot do that for I only saw her twice. She came to ask for my help and the second time came to pay me with the only coin she had. There,' she indicated the ear-rings. 'Put them on, my lady, they'll bring you luck.'

I did as she requested, arranging them by the kitchen mirror, as she drained her last cup of tea, gathered her basket. 'I must be on my way, now, my lady, bless you for your refreshment.'

'It's a long way to Dunbar, would you not like to rest here for a while?'

She shook her head. 'Nay, there are other calls I have still to make.'

'I'll walk with you to the end of the drive.'

She seemed pleased and as we reached the gates she said: 'Our camp is by Dunbar Castle. We leave there for Kirk Yetholm on the last night of the old year. There is a new king to be crowned.' She placed a hand on my arm. 'My lady, remember Dunbar – should you need friends or your own folk, you know where to find us.' She gave me an odd smile. 'Remember too when danger threatens those the gipsies love, they have many ways unknown to Gorgios of making them vanish into thin air.' She hung her head a little, avoiding my eyes, and her voice seemed a mere whisper of the wind from the sea. 'Remember – if you should ever have such need, we wait until the last night of the old year.'

'You are very kind,' I said, 'it isn't very likely, but if we are anywhere near Dunbar, then I'll certainly come and see you.' But even as I said the words, I felt a sudden chill at my heart, and told myself it was only to be expected standing in the bright cold autumn sunlight. 'Thank you for these,' I touched the ear-rings.

'Wear them in health and luck,' she said and took my hands

164

in both of hers. Closing her eyes, her lips moving silently in what was either spell or benediction. In that moment I was certain that she had lied about fortune-telling and that she saw the whole of my life spread out as clearly as the drive at Monkshall.

'I would like to know one thing before you go – in what way you were able to help my mother?'

She looked at me smiling. 'I wasn't – she must have changed her mind, anyway the camp moved on and her with it.'

'Then why did you keep her ear-rings all these years?'

'Because they were payment for a service I never gave her. They didn't belong to me.'

'What did she want?' My mind fluttered ahead to a love potion, a fortune telling, something sweet and innocently girlish.

Her glance was candid. 'She wanted me to rid her of her unborn baby. Many women, Gorgios too, came to me for I was famed for certain skills in such matters. However, fate or her own decision, willed it otherwise.'

'The baby?'

'The baby was yourself, my lady.'

And although I stood watching her, I was never conscious of the moment when she disappeared through the gates and when suddenly I remembered a dozen questions I wanted to ask, the road beyond Monkshall was empty.

There were no more dramas. Time moved on and the old year crept to a close. It was as if the old gipsy's advent set sharply the calendar to winter and the sky darkened while the birds and beasts and the gardens at Monkshall prepared for their sleep until spring. Inside the house, the gas jets burned noisily all day in the gloomy kitchen, where Mrs. Maxwell and the servants prepared puddings, meats, blackbun and shortbread for the approaching festive season.

At last the day of Rob's return dawned and despite the doctor's gloomy forecast, I had not needed to call him and I felt and looked a great deal stronger than I had at Rob's departure. I roamed the house, moving a cushion, straightening a picture, staring in every mirror as I did so –

'He's here – he's here.'

A rattle of wheels on the drive, the door opened and in one bound he was across the hall and I was in his arms again. An hour later we sat sedately by the drawing-room fire while Mrs. Maxwell brought in the tea, and it was just as if he had never been away.

When he remarked on how well I looked and admired my ear-rings, I was pleased. 'I hoped you would approve. As you know, I don't normally wear anything quite as large, as they only accentuate my gipsy appearance.'

'And what is wrong with that, I should like to know? I like my wife to look exotic. Remember it was that wild gipsy appearance that first drew me to you,' he added with a smile. 'Besides they look as if they belong to you.'

'And so in a way, they do.' I told him the story of the old gipsy woman. 'They seem to have acted like a talisman to my health.'

He nodded. 'So it seems – as if your mother's hand had reached out of the grave and given you a token – to apologise to the child she had not wanted.'

'And who cost her her life. I wonder what changed her mind about keeping me.'

'Or who changed her mind? Remember there must have been a man involved somewhere.'

'Then why did he desert her? Oh, Rob, there are so many questions to which I'll never know the answer. Did she have a premonition that in bearing me her own life would be forfeit – and then for some unknown reason, decided to continue carrying me? I've thought a thousand times of the sad circumstances of her life – '

'It was short, but perhaps she packed a great deal of love and happiness into it,' said Rob philosophically.

'I hope so.'

'And talking of love and happiness. We have a special

celebration – your birthday tomorrow and our first Christmas together.'

'Christmas has rarely been a happy time for me. I was often ill as a child then and missed all the parties and when I grew up – oh, I don't know, but it was *never* what I expected it to be.'

'My darling, you hadn't met me then. I promise you all your Christmases shall be happy from now on.'

I dared not tell him that I was constantly seeing the ghost of last Christmas, of Sir Andrew quarrelling with Willy Tyler, the Brownes waiting for a chance to blacken my name and getting their chance when Sir Andrew committed suicide and they destroyed his note to me. Would I ever forget it, reliving each day in painful detail? Would Monkshall ever allow me to forget the past? Perhaps going back to Faro was a shrewd move on Rob's part. Certainly if there were ever ill wishes at this time of goodwill, I was sure that the Brownes would do their best to convey them to me.

We drove into Edinburgh on the afternoon of Christmas Day. It was pleasantly mild with a threat of rain, as always the wind on Princes Street seeming stronger than anywhere else in Scotland. Edinburgh was *en fête,* and from our carriage the street was packed with other vehicles, while along Princes Street Gardens, which were being improved and the rather ugly recesses rearranged as grottos, children played encouraged by the mild day, proudly exhibiting to less fortunate children new toys and hoops. There were also children clustered around every toyshop and bazaar window, or else emerging from the doors their faces red with the excitement of clutching new treasures.

Stevenson House of Novelties was always specially popular at this time of year and there was a magic, an excitement about the occasion that recalled those of my own childhood and I saw myself in the many shrill laughing small girls, and Sir Andrew in their stately bearded guardians, trying to remain unconcerned and hold on to a shred of dignity in the midst of 'Come all ye faithful' sung by a Salvation Army band. All this combined with glittering lights inside shops and fairy grottos from which children emerged convinced that magic exists – how else to explain the mysterious parcel thrust into their hands by a jovial Santa Claus?

'Let's go inside,' said Rob.

There were mechanical toys of every kind for the Prince Consort had made German goods acceptable and popular too. 'Poupee' life-size dolls made by their craftsmen had china faces, eyes that opened and closed, beautiful human hair and smiling dimpled faces. They were very different from the wax dolls with their expressionless faces which were my childhood legacy and showed an alarming tendency to melt away when placed on a chair too near to the fire.

Exhilarated by the excitement Rob and I became like children ourselves, and shocked sober matrons and dignified gentlemen by winding up clockwork trains and dancing bears and drummer boys. Finally under the eagle and disapproving eyes of the shop assistant, a rather shame-faced Rob bought me a music box with a ballet dancer who pirouetted to the strains of a Chopin nocturne.

We dined at the Cafe Royal and returned home with my head on Rob's shoulder, for as on that first occasion, I had drunk a little too much wine and all our conversation was 'Do you remember – ?' As if we had known each other for half a century instead of being married for scarcely half a year. Next morning when I awoke in the great bed at Monkshall with Rob sleeping peacefully at my side, I was certain that this Christmas was going to be different, that my gloomy forecast was misplaced and I was indeed the luckiest woman in the world.

On Saturday evening, we joined a party of Rob's business friends and their wives at the pantomime 'Robinson Crusoe' in the Royal Princess Theatre. The press announcement of 'magnificent new scenery and tasteful costumes, sparkling music and magnificent transformation scene, representing the Dawn of the Flowers' had not been in the slightest way exaggerated. The ladies were all charming to me and by the end of the evening promises of further visits to each other's homes were exchanged.

Perhaps vanity was a fault, but I fancied that many surreptitious and admiring glances were bestowed on my husband, who always looked his best in evening dress, with black cape lined in red satin and a silver topped cane. I had to admit that I was one of the admirers too, that as far as I was concerned he was the handsomest man present.

'You were the toast of Edinburgh, my love,' he said as we rode home, 'we must go abroad in society a little more. Perhaps a series of dinner parties if you're feeling strong enough. I have no intentions of leaving you again before the baby arrives,' he kissed my hair, 'my darling, I miss you too greatly to go into voluntary exile from you – '

'Oh Rob, I have never been so happy. This is the happiest time of my whole life.'

Over breakfast next morning, Rob read the newspapers as was his habit and only the direst emergency admitted interruption.' Listen to this: "Mr. Edison, the American inventor, claims to have discovered an effective cheap electric light which is a perfect substitute for gas for domestic use." Think of it, Christina, next year at this time we might have just such a magical appliance, press a switch and hey presto. No more hazards of carrying oil lamps into rooms where there's no gas either.'

That afternoon was no way different to our usual Sunday in that as soon as lunch was cleared away, Rob went out to exercise the horses while I read by the fire. I must admit the visitor came upon me unexpectedly for I was apparently reading but in reality dozing, full of foolish dreams of a happiness I was beginning to believe could last for ever. But when I awoke my world had disappeared as if it had never existed except in the fantasy of my own heart.

A tap on the door. 'There's a gentleman here –' Mrs. Maxwell's voice.

A figure pushed her gently aside. 'It's all right, I'll announce myself. My dear Christina.' And Garnet Faro was bowing over my hand.

10

I was genuinely delighted to see him. 'Garnet, what a lovely surprise. Oh, you're looking so well.'

He was handsomer than ever, but had lost his ethereal looks. There was a suspicion of tough strength now that strangely enough suggested Rob. I wondered why I had ever had that first illusion that this one would not make old bones.

'Christina.' He clasped my hands to his breast. 'You are more beautiful than ever –'

'But tell me – how –'

'I won't beat about the bush. I'm just off a ship from London. When I graduated I took an engineering post in America. I have been extremely fortunate in some speculations and you'll be surprised to know that at twenty-two I am a man of property. I already have most of the material things I want in life.'

'How splendid.'

'Did you know that my mother left a letter to be opened after her death, telling me that the Captain was not my father? My own father to whom she was betrothed was his brother and died before I was born. Really, Christina, it's such a relief to know that I had not been unnaturally hating my real father –'

'Then don't you think you owe the Captain some gratitude for bringing you up in such circumstances, as his own son?' I asked gently.

'No, I don't think I owe him anything at all.' His frown was black, his voice sharp. 'Look at the way he treated my mother all those years. And imagine not allowing you to stay for her funeral. Such boorish behaviour. Oh, let's not talk about him.' His face became gentle again. 'Can you guess what brings me here?' And without waiting for my reply, he continued:

'I am on my way back to Faro. The Captain, too, has been away since my mother's death and as he has little interest in the property, I have a plan to make him hand over what is mine by moral right, seeing that my father was the elder son. I think he'll agree, he won't dare refuse,' he added grimly. Then smiling took my hands again. 'Christina, I have come to ask you to return to Faro with me.'

'Garnet – I can't. It's impossible.'

'Hear me out, please. I don't want you as housekeeper, I want you at Faro as its mistress.'

'I don't understand.'

'I think you do. You must be aware that I am deeply in love with you. In view of my wealth, I consider the difference in our ages unimportant – I have never been interested in young girls, anyway. And ever since I left America it was with one idea, that I should return to Faro and take you there, as my wife.'

I sat down. 'Garnet – I'm sorry.'

'Please, Christina. I know I can make you love me. I'll do anything in the world for you. At least give me a chance.'

'A chance – do you mean that you don't *know?* Garnet, my dear, I'm already married.'

He looked at me with stricken eyes, a child whose precious toy lies broken before his eyes. 'It can't be true. Why didn't the woman who let me in tell me? – I asked for Miss Holly,' he said stiffly. 'And now you've allowed me –'

'My dear Garnet, I had no idea of the purpose of your visit, or I should have told you immediately. You haven't given me much opportunity to say anything,' I added gently, wondering how I was going to add insult to injury by telling him the truth – and more urgently how I could get rid of him before Rob arrived. In that moment I saw the other Ruth Faro I had never known, the vindictive spoilt woman who had poisoned

172

her son's mind against the man who had been a father to him, despite the conditions of his birth.

'At least, now that I am here, perhaps I may have the privilege of meeting your husband.'

As he spoke, downstairs a door opened and closed. Footsteps, then handle turned, Rob crossed the room, took me in his arms. Then following my startled glance, he turned and saw Garnet.

'Garnet has just looked in, he's on his way back to Faro.'

Rob smiled. 'How were things in America?'

Garnet ignored his outstretched hand. 'Not so good as they were in Monkshall obviously,' he said drily.

Rob continued to smile. 'Will you be staying with us for a while? Help us bring in the New Year? Faro will be bleak and empty just now and Christina and I are in need of some excuse for a family occasion.'

I had never loved my husband more than at that moment. 'Yes, Garnet – please stay.'

He shook his head, eyes averted from us. 'I hardly think the Captain would welcome a skeleton at the feast. Especially as I came to claim a bride.'

'A bride?' asked Rob and looked quickly at me. 'I'm sorry, Garnet, I did write, but the letters were returned, your address unknown.'

I was aware of Garnet's close scrutiny and finding his glance rest and remain on my thickened waistline, instinctively I put my hands over my stomach.

'So that's the way of it. Very interesting,' he said with an ugly smile. 'So there's to be a legitimate heir and doubtless the bastard of Faro will be disinherited.'

'While advising you to watch your tongue, young man, I would also say that I have nothing of the sort in mind. I intend offering you Monkshall since Christina and I shall be returning to Faro once the baby arrives.'

'It is imminent then?' asked Garnet.

'Not until spring. We were married in July,' I said nervously.

173

'Of course you were, unless you were adding bigamy to your other crimes. But the child might have been conceived long before that.'

'And what the devil are you implying?' demanded Rob.

'Rob,' I said warningly, watching the white set of his face.

'I mean,' said Garnet, 'that I'm getting a very clear picture for the first time of my poor mother's death. How very convenient. The Captain here has a wife who is something of an encumbrance. He chances to hear of a murder trial, visits perhaps by curiosity but more likely, with the dawn of an interesting possibility in mind –'

I saw Rob's face tighten, his hands clench.

'The lady is acquitted – the verdict "Not proven" – and suddenly the gallant Captain sees the perfect way to rid himself of an unwanted wife. He will lure the young woman to Faro, befriend and then seduce her, and having her thoroughly in his power, he will persuade her with promises of marriage to help him get rid of his wife, in exactly the same manner as her guardian died. Neat, isn't it?'

Rob said nothing. I looked at him, willing him to deny it.

'You must agree, Christina,' said Garnet. 'It was the perfect solution. There was one unfortunate aspect, my mother's letter stating that the Captain was not my father. So to provide myself against the lean years that might lie ahead, I took – certain steps –'

'Such as?' asked Rob quietly.

'Such as a certain bottle of Tonic Coffee Cordial which the gallant Captain used to bring home for his ailing wife. From South America.'

I saw Rob stiffen. 'My God – that was only opium to ease her pain.'

'Precisely. As I discovered when I had the contents analysed.'

'You mean that you suspected I was trying to kill her?'

'The thought had crossed my mind. I must confess I was disappointed to learn that far from a lethal dose, she would

174

have had to drink a whole bottle at once for such an unfortunate result. However, opium is a common drug, there's plenty of it to be obtained through my medical friends and I'm afraid I took a few liberties with the contents of your excellent Tonic Coffee Cordial. Both yourself – and in due course the procurator-fiscal – will no doubt be surprised at the now lethal dose of opium it contains.'

'You unprincipled little bastard.'

'Rob!'

He shook off my restraining hand. 'Don't you see what he's up to? Well, you won't blackmail me, I'll see you in hell first!' He made a swift movement towards Garnet who stood his ground smiling.

'If you don't find yourself there first – at the end of a rope, you'd better listen carefully to what I have to say. I have the cordial and you have Christina and an unborn child. Let's say we are about equal. So in fair exchange for the bottle, you may give me Faro.'

'I will not give you one damned inch of Faro.'

'Oh yes, I think you will, once you've had time to think about it. If not for yourself, at least spare a thought for your blushing bride. Remember in the eyes of the law which has an unfortunately long memory, she is regarded as not unskilled in the art of administering overdoses and disposing of some person who might stand in her way. Remember that verdict – not proven. Think what might be accomplished if it could be proved that she was your mistress before she ever set foot in Faro and cultivated my mother's friendship and trust. Imagine my mother's body brought from her vault, and the contents of her stomach revealing evidence of opium –'

'You damned ghoul – your poor mother was dying –'

'But the law wouldn't look kindly – nor would the church – upon the hint that someone might have helped her into eternity. Please don't interrupt – imagine any procurator-fiscal being presented again with the precise circumstances of those which attended Sir Andrew's death.' He shook his head. 'Don't you think he would be ominously impressed? A not very enviable future for Christina, her child or yourself, I'm afraid. Connivance, accessory to murder – it's all there, waiting to be proved – and by God, unless you give me what I want, I'm going to prove it.'

'Garnet, please, I beg of you – I thought you loved me.'

'Love you, Christina, of course I love you. But not as much as I hate him. There is no emotion in this world so strong as my hatred for Captain Cawdor Faro. And if I don't get him hanged, then it won't be for lack of trying.'

He was still smiling when Rob hit him. For a moment he lay still, blood trickling from his lip, eyes closed. I thought he was dead until Rob dragged him to his feet and flung him into a chair. 'Now listen to me, you ungrateful pup – I've done my best for you, no real father could have done more. I married your mother who pretended to love me, so that I could give you a name. In those early days, she had nothing but scorn for me. It wasn't until she was ill and knew she was dying that she saw fit, God help her, to repent to the extent of craving my love, which she had repulsed. It was too late for that, too late to repair the damage she had done, poisoning a child's mind against me, as part of her revenge.'

He was silent for a moment, looking almost with pity at the cowering figure in the chair. 'Well, I'm finished with you now, as I should have done years ago – with you and your mother. When I arrive back at Faro, I don't want to find you there – I never want to set eyes on you again – if I do, by God, I'll kill you. Now get out of my house and do your worst. We aren't afraid of a miserable little swine like you –'

*　　　*　　　*　　　*

Like some terrible prophecy of doom, as soon as he departed we became aware of the storm. As if to remind us that we were frail transient mortals whose lives could be brushed off like so many insects from a leaf in the garden, and that as such we

176

had little right to expect happiness as our normal condition. All night long it raged deriding us. The wind screamed against the windows, like avenging hands trying to reach us, the rain lashed down in a melancholy unending dirge. Occasionally there were other sounds – of roof-tiles hurtling down, of trees splintering.

We went to bed like two frightened children, fearfully whispering and lying wide-eyed in the darkness. Somewhere during the night I came to a decision which did not make any particular sense, but at least seemed to contribute action, a deliberate move to escape the net that I felt closing in around us. One thing shone abundantly clear. I could never endure another prison cell, another trial. I had spent all my strength on the first one, there was nothing left in me with which to fight again.

Useless for Rob to try to console me. If Garnet was speaking the truth and had tampered with the contents of the coffee cordial, in view of the unholy coincidence of my past history, it was certain that no second jury would acquit us or deliver another verdict of 'Not proven'.

Then to have my baby in prison. The thought was so monstrous I knew I would die. Whether I survived its birth or not, my heart would fail me and I should surely die of grief.

Hollow-eyed with lack of sleep, Rob left for Leith next morning to attend to various matters concerning his ship. Having made up my mind, I let him go with more composure than imagination ever suggested I possessed.

Swiftly I packed together a valise and wrote him a short letter stating that if Garnet did indeed proceed with the accusation, once the baby was safely born, I would return and face trial. I told him I loved him – always had and always would, and that he was not to try to find me.

Mrs. Maxwell was engaged in another part of the house, and if any of the servants witnessed my departure they would imagine I was meeting the Captain. And so began my vigil for the south-bound coach, some distance from Monkshall. I was going to Dunbar, certain that the gipsy woman had always known I would come, that she had seen clearly the pattern of what lay ahead, and that her advent into my life was no chance encounter, but that my mother's hand had stretched out from the grave, through her, to warn me.

If there was solace to be found in my distress, it was that I was returning to my mother's people, who had promised a refuge and would take good care of me. As I looked back towards Monkshall, the idea persisted that I would see it no more, that I would die in childbirth and my child – and Rob's – would be brought up as a gipsy, and for me one of the circles of which all life is secretly formed would be full-turned. Destiny, fate – God – whatever name one calls the Master by, would be satisfied.

I tried not to think of Rob. At least by withdrawing from his life I had made the chance of his arrest and imprisonment unlikely. He could show the authorities my confession of guilt. However foolish and irrational my behaviour sounds, standing on that bleak empty road waiting for the coach, with tears rolling down my cheeks, I believed what I was doing was best for both of us by averting the noose even temporarily from around our necks.

Oh, it was all so unfair. Was it right that I should have to go away, to turn my back on the life which had seemed so happy? Was it unreasonable that I should expect some joy after my past sufferings?

But even while I asked myself these questions, I knew my reason for flight was self-interest. I was running away from the terror of imprisonment, of being caged like an animal in a small cell, cut off from all I loved in the world.

The day was in keeping with the leaden weight at my heart, and as I paced back and forth to keep warm, I hoped the coach would arrive before Rob's return, before he had a chance to read my letter. Time passed and the road was briefly occupied by occasional riders and private carriages. negotiating the fallen branches which remained as a token of the gale's fury. The rain began with renewed frenzy and increasingly cold and uncomfortable, my stomach began to ache ominously. Another horseman galloped past, cloak flying, then suddenly he reined to and trotted back.

'Been waiting long? Am I right in thinking you're waiting for the south coach? Aye well, lass, I saw it mired down in a flooded road several miles back – just out of Edinburgh. And once they get it out of there they'll find trees down all the way along. I hear tell there's a bridge collapsed further north in the gale. You'd best return to your home, lass,' he added, considering my bedraggled appearance and shabby valise, probably thinking I was a servant returning to my employer after the Christmas festivities. 'There'll be no coach till night.'

'How can I get to Dunbar?'

He shook his head. 'I dinna ken, lass. It's no' my way, or I'd take you on the saddle here.'

As he disappeared a familiar figure appeared from the direction of Monkshall. It was Rob, very white about the lips. His cheeks were wet with more than the rain. He had been crying, and when silently he lifted me into the saddle in front of him I felt the echo of the convulsion of grief that had shaken him. 'Thank God I found you. No, not a word until we are home.'

Later as I sat up in bed, with a roaring fire in the grate and sipping a hot drink, he said: 'I read your letter. What's it all about, Christina?'

'I was afraid that the wine was poisoned that night when I arrived at Faro and you said you would put her out of her misery and free us to marry, and that it would be nothing as you had killed an animal suffering less. Well, just in case, I poured your wine away and gave her the Coffee Cordial. She wanted something sweet and kept asking for more. She had three glasses, Rob—undiluted. Maybe I killed her!'

He was silent, and then said: 'I'm not sure that such a large dose would have made any difference – remember what Garnet said. Besides the body gets used to drugs after a

179

while. However, if Garnet goes ahead with the enquiry and an exhumation order reveals a large amount of opium in the stomach contents, once he reminds them about Sir Andrew's death, I'm afraid things will go ill with us both.'

'There must be some way to prove our innocence, if only we could think of it.'

He put his arms around me. 'Well, it doesn't lie in running away from me. Don't ever do that again. You know, I was quite prepared to come to Dunbar and vanish with you.'

'So you guessed – I might have known.'

'I'm serious about vanishing too, if the worst happens. I was investigating the possibilities at Leith this morning. We can take a ship to London, then to South America – we have a whole continent to disappear into – and I have enough money abroad, thank heaven, to start a new and not uncomfortable life. If only I were sure about the baby, and that you could safely endure a long sea voyage.'

'I'm so much stronger now, Rob – and doctors can be wrong. A gipsy caravan, a ship – or prison. It doesn't seem a very attractive alternative.'

'In that case, my darling, we had better make plans – '

But we never did. A loud rap on the front door, footsteps and voices.

I seized Rob's hands. 'The police?'

It was too late for flight. The door opened and Mrs. Maxwell announced Mr. Mackintosh. The old advocate was out of breath, obviously agitated. 'You must forgive this intrusion, I'm afraid the matter is of considerable urgency –'

Were we too late? Had the police already been informed? Only such an exigency could have brought the old man to us in such distress. I darted a look at Rob, who went calmly to the table and poured a glass of brandy which he handed to Mr. Mackintosh, with an invitation to be seated.

After a few sips, he looked at us both appealingly, as if he searched for words and wished us to assist him, then clearing his throat he began:

180

'Last night I had a visit from a distraught young man, the son of an esteemed client, who told me a curious story about a lady of whom he was enamoured and how she had been trapped into murder and subsequent marriage by an evil older man. The young man had evidence within his possession to prove murder, or at least accessory to murder, but as a last resort came to me to see if I could find extenuating circumstances which would incriminate the man yet save the young woman, whom he regarded as the mere victim of her passions.

'As our talk proceeded I began to realise that all was not what it seemed to be with this young man, and from several searching questions I discovered that there were less reputable motives than love for his dead mother. There was black hatred for the other man, considerable jealousy and some tampering with evidence was indicated, amounting to what the court would consider perjury.

'Eventually I lost my temper. I have little patience with blackmailers. I told him he must go ahead and see justice done. If he had evidence then he must present it to the procurator-fiscal and the young lady must take her chance. It was a stormy disagreeable night, and although hospitality and regard for his parent suggested that I should offer him a bed for the night, I was so desperate to be rid of his odious presence that, pretending I had a dinner engagement elsewhere, I took him in my carriage to Waverley Station and saw him and his luggage bestowed on the train to Dundee, at which station he would change for Aberdeen. He was still trying to enlist my aid as the train drew out, begging me to think of some means by which he could save the young woman while destroying the man, and I totally failed to make him see that such a course was immoral.'

He paused, mopped his forehead and took a few more sips of brandy. I hardly dared breathe, sitting up in bed, staring stiffly ahead, trying to control my hands from trembling. I hardly dare glance at Rob either, and when with great effort I did so, I encountered a stony, expressionless face.

181

Mr. Mackintosh took a rolled newspaper from his pocket. 'Have you, sir, seen this?'

Rob indicated our newspapers still folded on the breakfast tray unopened. 'I'm afraid not. I had urgent matters to attend –'

'Then I should advise you to open it,' said Mr. Mackintosh excitedly, and, donning his spectacles, unfolded the paper and read:

'Terrific Hurricane. Appalling Catastrophe at Dundee. Tay Bridge Down. Passenger Train hurled into River. Supposed loss of 200 lives. The scene at Tay Bridge Station tonight is simply appalling. Many thousands of persons are congregated around the building, and strong men and women are wringing their hands in despair . . .'

He laid it aside. 'There is much more,' and added with a sigh. 'There is not the shadow of doubt, I'm afraid, that the unfortunate young man is among those who perished.' He paused. 'I thought you might both be interested – and er, consoled, by my little drama, for there is not the slightest reason to suppose that I am not as responsible for this young man's death – murder, if you will – as my two friends were for his unhappy mother's demise.' He cleared his throat. 'I find the words difficult, I am trying to say that in both cases fate or God Almighty decided the issue and the human instrument for execution had neither yea nor nay to plead in the matter.'

We had yet to learn that our anxieties far from being at an end, with Garnet's unhappy exit from the world via the Tay Bridge, were only just beginning. The newspapers next morning announced that the original supposed loss of two hundred souls had been an exaggeration. A check made upon the ticket office had revealed that seventy-four passengers had joined the train en route.

Rob threw down the paper and said he must leave for Dundee immediately. As next-of-kin it would be expected of him to be there to await identification of Garnet's body. I begged to accompany him but he insisted I remain at Monkshall. I did so reluctantly, knowing that I should never have a moment's peace of mind until he returned and Garnet was safely buried in the vault at Faro. Yet I was not completely heartless, I was torn between pity for the young life I had seen that first day at Faro as doomed. Pity for his horrible death mingled with terror that he might return unscathed and destroy us.

So each day I waited restlessly for Rob to return with news that the whole melancholy business was at an end, while gathering from the newspapers that such was not to be, for the River Tay showed a certain reluctance in relinquishing its dead. Imagination painted hideous visions of trapped passengers still alive fighting for a way out of their watery tombs and only one body, that of an elderly woman was recovered within the first week while the flotsam from broken carriages began to float to the surface with a leisurely regularity.

From the beaches around Dundee there was more personal flotsam as the pathetic possessions of the dead fought their way to the surface, revealed as a Balmoral bonnet, a child's cotton sock and felt hat, a velvet shoe, a cap with paint stains and a woman's chemise. These items and many more were deposited in the refreshment room at Tay Bridge station which was equipped with tables for that melancholy purpose and all in due course, were seized upon to be identified by weeping relatives, who knew by this last token that the miracle they prayed for by which their loved one had escaped the catastrophe, must be put aside for ever.

'In this gay and festive season, we must deplore the loss of life,' announced the compassionate ballad-sellers, while the stern Sabbatarians from pulpits the length and breadth of Scotland denounced the godless Sunday travellers in sermons stating that: 'The fall of the bridge is a judgement to be classed with the wars in Afghanistan and Zululand as a token of God's displeasure.'

Rob returned to Monkshall every few days from his vigil in the Royal Hotel, Dundee. Pale and drawn he recalled the

183

horrors of waiting among the stricken weeping relatives by the sullen water above which the ghastly parody of twisted girders was all that remained of the once-handsome bridge.

'Almost every person I encountered on the streets or in my hotel seemed to be in mourning dress, walking swiftly, white-faced, head bowed in grief. It was as if the whole town mourned that there was not a household who had not lost some member of the family on that train. When it was known that I had lost a son, my only son, kindness was heaped upon me from every quarter. My attempts to withdraw, to keep my own counsel were mistaken for natural grief, instead of inward jubilation. For as the days passed and the hearts of these poor people were wrung and broken with sorrow, my own heart rejoiced, for the disaster which shattered their worlds only served to make yours and mine secure. Their deaths brought us the promise of life.'

At the end of January, Rob said there was no point in returning to Dundee. Only thirty-three of the seventy-four missing had been recovered, and as Rob's extensive enquiries at Faro and among Garnet's University friends known to him revealed that they had expected his arrival from America around Christmastime, it laid at rest our fears that some change of heart occasioned by his conversation with Mr. Mackintosh had made him leave the train before it reached the bridge.

'Had he decided to visit friends en route, he would certainly have reappeared somewhere by now,' said Rob consolingly.

I wished I could be sure as January passed into February and only occasional bodies floated to the surface, to be identified by relatives and quickly buried. The newspaper men had drifted off to other stories and Dundee life proceeded with interest stirring momentarily when the tides continued to yield their burden of flotsam.

During the weeks while Rob was in Dundee, I had lived in constant nightmare that Garnet would walk in unannounced to taunt me. And when Rob returned, each time the front-doorbell rang we were certain that the unexpected caller was the police. Then one day we received through the post a small package with a note from the authorities, saying that a child on the beach at Broughty Ferry had found the enclosed glittering among the sea-weed.

Rob opened the parcel, took out a rather battered gold watch, inscribed 'Cawdor Faro'. Once the possession of his grandfather, he had given it to Garnet on his eighteenth birthday. It had stopped at 7.16 and was all the evidence we were to have that Garnet's body was one of the twenty-nine in a grave of mud and sand at the bottom of the Firth of Tay. In due course, he was pronounced dead and Rob's enquiries about his business dealings in America produced evidence of a fortune much more modest than he had claimed. However, reluctant to touch a penny, Rob used it to endow a convalescent home at Monkshall for the widows and orphans of Merchant Sailors.

Soon after our arrival at Faro in early April, our son made his debut into the world. After all our early misgivings and perhaps in compensation for what we had both suffered, his birth was an easy one, from which I made a sufficiently speedy recovery to present Rob with two more sons before Cawdor had reached school-age.

A contented happy life? Yes, except on nights when the sea hurls itself against the rocks under Faro and the waters moan in the underground caves like the cries of a drowning man, when the seagulls scream derision and hurtle, echoing their laments, into a darkened sky. It is then that unease begins again, that the heart quakes and the ready smile fades, shrouding in momentary doubt the future that apparently lies, mild and clear, golden as the sands stretching to a sunlit sea below the House of Faro.

Then nightmare asks the one inescapable question: Are we safe for ever – or, will he someday return?